"QALANDAR"

EARTH NEEDED A SUPERHERO

by:

FRAZ AHMED

Disclaimer

This is a work of fiction. Names, characters, businesses, places, events, locales and incidents are either the products of the author's imagination or used in a fictious manner. Any resemblance to actual persons, living or dead, or actual events is purely coincidental.

TABLE OF CONTENTS

Author's Introduction

I grew up inspired by the Hollywood movies and music. Action, romance and science fiction have always been my top choice. I enjoy being fascinated for days after watching good action and superhero movies.

As I grew older, I realized that almost every human on earth is seeking peace and many of them keep waiting for a Messiah (Superhero), who can magically remove their pain and problems.

Moreover, I love travelling and learning about different cultures and human behaviors. I am a travel & life style blogger (perspectives.life) and a content writer.

SCENE I

As the first rays of sunlight peeked over the horizon, a soft voice sang through the air. Birds nested and huddled for warmth during the cold night awoke to the singing. Perched on branches, they joined along with the sweet tune— the sound of azan played for the world to hear.

The large wooden doors of the mosque opened. Men adorned in black caps filed into the courtyard that had become a snow-filled wonderland. Ice trickled down from tall chir pines. And the winds whipped and whistled through the crowd. But even the chilling frost was no deterrent for those who wished to walk alongside the towering forests of Kashmir.

Breaking free from the crowd, a man with sleek black hair and a well-groomed beard, Ali, traveled along the road breathing warm air into his gloves. He was well-equipped for the cold— thick blue jeans, a fitted cotton polo, and an insulated coat protected his body from the elements. His calming brown eyes looked through the trees and watched wild hares hop into snowdrifts. The nature of Pakistan was something he loved dearly.

But calm days such as these hadn't been the norm. Though tensions with India had long seemed dormant, Ali remained worried for his family. His mind returned to the headlines he had read; the ever-growing crime in the cities was something he couldn't ignore. Ali shook his head, *"With such a beautiful world, why are there those who seek to destroy it?"*

His home, Kashmir, had always been a bone of contention between Pakistan and India. Both countries wanted to claim the land as their own. And since 1947, both fought four wars in hopes of taking Kashmir for themselves. Even with UN intervention, the border came to be known as the Line of Control— the point in which no one could truly believe they were safe.

It was only a short drive to the mountains from his home. And while those trails and forests were filled with the beauty of nature, war left them ridden with wire fences and mines. One needed to proceed with caution.

As he was lost in his thoughts, Ali noticed a figure moving by the edge of the road. He jogged ahead and what he found was an innocent life left to suffer. Capable of only the faintest whimper, the baby deer looked at the man. Kneeling down beside the young animal, Ali placed his hand on a bright red gash. Whatever truck had hit the deer was long gone, but Ali knew it was only a short walk back to his home.

Scooping the deer up into his arms, he jogged along a picket-fence that led to a large barn with thick panels of stained wood. Upon swinging open the doors, Ali was greeted by a large chestnut stallion with a mane that flowed like silk. The horse whinnied aloud as Ali brought the baby deer to a clean stall. And after laying the wounded animal onto a fleece blanket, he brushed his fingers against the horse's coat.

"It's okay, Tiger. You have a new friend," he said to the horse before feeding him a fresh carrot from the barrels.

The horse nudged against Ali's hand, graciously accepting the treat. But Ali's focus was on the deer whose breathing had become shallow. Sifting through crates of feed and supplies, he found a first-aid kit and took it to the young animal.

With wounds so deep, he feared what more pain the deer may feel if he attempted to suture the gash. In the kit, he found a syringe with a sedative. Ali pet the deer to calm him as he administered the injection.

"When you wake up, you'll feel better than ever," he whispered.

His eyes locked onto the deer. At that moment, he sensed calmness in the animal's gaze. Without understanding any of each other's words, the two were able to know how each other felt. Flickering his eyes shut, the deer rested.

Moments like these were the very reason Ali had built his barn. It was a home for his beloved horse, but also a place to care for the animals of the forest. Sparrows nestled at the barn floor as Ali spread seed for the local bird to eat. He welcomed all in need to his home.

After bandaging the deer's wound, Ali gave one last pat to his horse. Among animals was somewhere he felt comfortable. But as he looked out of the barn to a ranch-style house with an open garage, he knew that there were others whom he wished to care for as well.

SCENE II

Cedarwood siding fitted the home's exterior. Ali stepped through the cobblestone walkway that led to the garage. His garden— manicured with trimmed lawn and pines had turned white with snow. His eyes turned back to the forest before he entered his home; he had to wonder if there was a mother deer somewhere in those depths searching for her child.

But before Ali had a moment longer to ponder, he was greeted by his wife at the door. Mehwish smiled as she saw him. Her lips were like rose petals and when she showed joy, that expression traveled up to her doe-like olive eyes.

She tilted her delicate round chin, motioning towards the darkened stain on Ali's coat. He smiled back at her and shrugged. It was no secret to her that her husband cared for all life around him. And if anything, it caused her to feel even more loved to have a husband with a heart as large as Ali's.

As Ali walked down the hall to shower, Mehwish prepared the morning's breakfast. On the stove, she fried eggs and flatbreads made of wheat. Hearing a metallic chime, she rushed to the toaster to retrieve four golden slices of toast and placed them on a dish along with an assortment of jam.

Mehwish brought the plates out to the table where her two children sat— her eight-year-old daughter Rabia and four-year-old son Sami. Hearing the water from the shower stop, she called out to him, inviting him to a warm home-cooked meal.

Ali, though, paused in front of his wardrobe. As he pulled a dark-blue polo over his head, his hand pressed against the scar that stretched across his chest. After so many years, it still hadn't healed. And he was reminded of that day every time he saw it. But that, nor anything, was going to stop him from enjoying breakfast with his family.

Upon entering the dining room, he was immediately greeted by his daughter, Rabia. She wrapped her arms around him as he patted her gently on the head. Ali looked to his young son, Sami. The boy tossed his utensils in the air and exclaimed aloud as he saw his father. Ali smiled back at him; seeing his children's faces filled him with joy.

"Good morning... good morning!" came from a long wooden cage.

An African Grey parrot sat perched on a large branch eating a piece of fruit. Mehwish laughed as she watched the bird sing and flutter his wings. She sat down and helped Sami eat his breakfast, cutting small pieces of flatbread and assisting his hand as he held his fork.

"His next session is tomorrow morning. I think you were right. He's going to hit all of his goals from the last meeting. It's been hard, but he's getting better," Mehwish said.

Seeing a smile spread onto his young son's face, Ali was relieved. Sami had come a long way from the day the doctor diagnosed him with autism. It was too early to tell if the boy would speak his first words soon. But Ali saw improvements in Sami's temperament alone and happiness was what he wanted for his children most of all.

Ali kissed his son's forehead before turning back towards his wife. It was difficult for him to keep his eyes off of her. The beauty she had was inside and out. He was thankful to have such a caring wife and that his children could have such a loving mother. As he smiled at her, her warm cheeks glowed red. He wished to make her feel like a queen and judging by the way her green eyes sparkled, he believed it was a success.

Taking the final bite of his jam-covered toast, Ali beckoned to Rabia and the two headed for the doorway. With his grip on the door handle, he turned back to his wife.

"I love you. Take care of yourself," he said to her as he led his daughter outside.

A yellow bus idled outside of Ali's home. Waiting in a car across the road were the neighbors— Fariha, a single mother and her daughter, Hiba. Rabia called out to the neighbor and the two jogged towards the bus. While the newspapers mongered fear, Ali was thankful to have such good neighbors around him.

Waving to the bus driver, Ali watched his daughter and her friend leave for school. He knew that he, too, needed to set off on the road for work. Breathing in the crisp morning air, all was calm. But his eyes drifted back to the barn, not all was in the clear.

SCENE III

Adjusting his hardhat, Ali walked down the halls and watched through the glass into the factory. Bulbs glided down a conveyor belt, heated by blue flames until they reached a rack where workers checked for any imperfections. Watching the progress, Ali was satisfied with his team's work.

He filled out his daily report— each shipment of lightbulbs was checked and ready to be loaded onto the trucks. While an uneventful workday, Ali was pleased that there had been no accidents and all of the day's quotas had been met.

With his clipboard in hand, Ali knocked on his boss's door who welcomed him with a handshake and motioned for him to sit down. Since Ali had begun working at the factory, his team had always been on time with their goals and not once was any protocol violated.

And that wasn't over-confidence on Ali's part but the words of his boss himself.

"This is great work. You've been consistent every day and even your team has nothing but good words to say about you. Tell you what. After lunch, take the rest of the day off. I'll have the shipping department take over from here."

Ali smiled. He worked hard and his efforts were paying off. The earlier he could return home from work, too, the earlier he could check on the young deer, he thought. And it had been quite some time since he had caught up with friends.

His boss motioned towards the door and the two men set off towards the cafeteria. Still early, not many had yet arrived. But the boss spotted and greeted his long-time friend while Ali noticed a young man who had started working at the factory just a few weeks prior.

Not being one to ease the volume of his voice, the boss boasted to his friend about Ali, "Ten years he's worked for me and there's not been a single complaint. I'm telling you, Ali is a superhero in disguise. He makes my job so much easier!"

Laughing and shaking his head, Ali sat across from the young worker. Saleem was his name; he was a shorter man with rounder features, a thin beard, and quaffed black hair. From the skittish and squirrel-like expression on the man's face, Ali could tell that something was troubling him.

"It's my mother," Saleem said, "She's been so sick. I want to buy her medicine but… well, there's still a week until the salaries come in and-"

Before Saleem could say another word, Ali reached for his wallet and pulled out a thousand-rupee bill. The young man's eyes grew wide as he took the paper note. He expressed his thanks profusely, and Ali only asked that he paid back once the salary day had come.

Overhearing his boss again, Ali became uncomfortable, "He's an honest man. That's what I like about him. But… well, between you and me, I think he has a heavy heart."

Ali gulped as he heard the next words, "He was in the army back in the day. But from what I hear, he was court-martialed."

SCENE IV

Fair winds blew across the windshield sending snowflakes flowing like whirling dancers. The front wipers on Ali's SUV kept his vision clear, but his mind was distracted. Both hands were clenched on his steering wheel. The words of his boss were still lingering on his mind as he drove.

Though, just like his SUV continued to carry him through extreme heat and cold, he carried himself through anything that life threw his way. Rust could form on the doors and he'd be there to sand and repaint the metal before any corrosion. But just as his old SUV needed regular repair, he, too, needed to give himself time to unwind.

On his way home from work, Ali parked along the roadside beside a sedan. Flags in vibrant shades of burning red and cool, calming blue outlined a trail that led to a shrine. Ali looked at the green walls. But he remained seated in his vehicle. In his mind, there was still skepticism.

He was aware of what some believed. The shrines— graves of those who lived pious lives —were places where one could talk to the spirits who would relay those messages to God. Those, though, were only the beliefs of others. He was uncertain if it were something he could trust.

While it wasn't a place he often prayed, Ali knew it was a place where others in need would gather. Those seeking charity would sit outside the holy place in hopes of the rich sharing some of their food or wealth. Ali's income was modest, but he believed he had enough to still give.

There was no one seated outside the shrine, but as Ali watched the door slide open he caught a glimpse of a tall figure walking into the snow. A man with long tasseled hair and a thick beard— Hassan. The two men made eye contact and Hassan approached the SUV.

His purple eyes shined bright as he extended his hand, "It's good to see you, friend."

Ali shook his friend's hand. Ice chilled their faces but it was nothing that could deter the reunion of two friends. Ali had noticed the sedan and he knew Hassan's beliefs. With his early day home from work, Ali thought it would be a good opportunity to reconnect with a friend.

SCENE V

Smoke billowed from the chimney of the tea shop. The sun had just begun to set, leaving the streets dark save for the warm yellow light that came from the shop. It was a cozy place downtown, but one that many would frequent to sit and enjoy the company of friends and family.

A shrill whistle came from a kettle. The aroma within the shop was rich with a hint of sweetness. Spicy chai, fresh honey, and dried berries filled Ali's nostrils as he poured steaming water in his cup. He breathed in the comforting scent and stared out at the darkness outside the window.

Inside, he and Hassan were comforted by light—wooden fixtures cast a yellow glow. But outside, between the setting sun and the heavy snowflakes falling down from the sky, sight was difficult. All who sat inside were escaping the winter world for something warm and calming.

As Hassan pulled his cup to his lips, Ali spoke to him, "How is your father? Is he well?"

"I have given charity to the shrine. I give food; I spread flowers on the grave. Even new cloth-"

Ali interjected, "Listen. I don't believe in these things."

When Ali visited the shrines, he did so to help those in need. But at the same time, he was unable to share the same beliefs that they had. It wasn't that he was unwilling, but he was unable to comprehend something he could not see. He did not deny the spirits within the graves, but when one had God in their heart, he did not see a need to speak one's prayers to any other.

"God is much nearer to us than our own heart. Another soul doesn't need to listen to what we can tell God ourselves. You've been trying to convince me about your spiritualism and Sufism for some time now. But I believe what I have been given. And what I am given, it will be by God."

Hassan smiled. He understood how Ali felt, but that didn't prevent him from having his own beliefs. It was true that God was all-knowing. Though, there was a power in the shrines that he knew was sacred. The lives of those buried within the shrines were pious and pure.

Ali continued, "You go alone to the top of the mountain. And I've seen so many shrines that you've visited. I just don't see any benefit. While you are gone, your father is sick and alone in his home. He needs you. Helping and caring for your father should be your duty."

"I have no one else but you as my friend," Hassan said as he set down his cup, "You take care of my father more than I do. Do you remember eight years ago when I had an accident and I was lying there moving towards death at the bank of a river? There were thousands of people looking at me and it was only you who offered help."

Lowering his eyes, Ali thought back to that day. He was in disbelief back then and even as time went by, he still didn't fully understand what happened that day. All he knew was that a man was injured and no one else was moving a finger to help him.

"Only you picked me up and took me to the hospital. You bore the expenses of my treatment. And you stayed there for two days until I came back to consciousness"

Ali nodded, "Of course. You had no ID and you were badly wounded."

"Yes. I remember everything. I still remember your voice in my ear while you were requesting the doctor. 'This is a human,' you said. 'Save him first. You will get the ID later.' It's been eight years and we are still friends."

A smile spread across Ali's face, "Eight years and you're still the same. You still climb the mountains alone and you cross the rivers. I get worried that a similar accident will happen again. You should stop chasing those Green Darwaish. It will cause you to lose your life."

It wasn't the Darwaish themselves that worried Ali. But Hassan's fixation on them was to the point of obsession. Often, he would pray at their shrines and to the spirits— those who had led pious lives seeking only knowledge and to assist the creatures of God.

Hassan held his teacup tightly in his hands, "Look, Ali. You were in the army."

Those words alone made Ali uncomfortable— sweat built at the back of his neck. But Hassan continued, "I know you don't like to talk about it, but I know what happened back in 1965. In the war between Pakistan and India, the Green Darwaish helped us. Haven't you heard those who admit that a green army came to help Pakistan? Everyone asks, 'Where did the green army come from?'"

Ali sighed, "I've heard the story, but I've never seen it. I can not be sure about it. It's never happened again. No one has mentioned another green army. Whatever that chapter was, it's finished. It's been over fifty years since then. You should focus on your future. Your age is passing. You can't even get married."

Seeing his friend's laugh was a relief, but Ali meant the words he said. Whatever had happened back then—

whatever people *said* happened back then was all but a legend. And Ali had reality to contend with. His family and those he cared about were more important to him than chasing something which he could not confirm himself.

SCENE VI

Parking in his garage, Ali looked at his garden. He recalled the rose bush bloomed every Spring and seldom in the Autumn. Though it was far too cold, he wished to see those vibrant red petals once more. He knew they were his wife's favorite and he loved seeing the way her cheeks would blush that same shade of red.

He walked back to the barn, eyeing up the bush. He told himself that the very first bloom of Spring would be a gift he would give to Mehwish. For being his beautiful wife, he wished to give her something to remind her of how dear she was to his heart.

Opening the barn door, he first checked on the young deer. His horse had already begun to rest for the night and the dense forest by his home was quiet. The silent night and cold chilling air were calming to Ali, but he had to worry about the animal in his care.

Checking the wound, the sutures were holding up and the gash appeared to be healing. The deer's breathing was shallow, but he was still asleep— resting and regaining his strength. Ali brought water for him to drink for when he awoke and rose to return to his home.

Just as he exited the barn, Ali heard a faint thump against the wood. He looked down to see a rabbit inching towards him. Ali bent down and extended his hand, inviting her to come forward. She was skittish, but Ali's movements were still and she chose to trust him.

As he watched the rabbit come near, he noticed four sets of tiny eyes behind her. The rabbit's children had joined her. Ali smiled as he returned to the barn to rummage through his store of carrots. The mother rabbit was the first to approach him and soon after, the young bunnies hopped into Ali's lap.

Moments like those filled Ali with joy. To be able to give and help all of God's creatures, it was what made life so precious in his eyes. He looked back to the deer. It broke his heart knowing that such a young animal was in such pain. But just as he had always done, Ali believed he would give whatever he could to help.

SCENE VII

Rabia rolled the dice— a four. She cheered, exclaiming aloud as she moved her token up the ladder and to the final one-hundredth square. After three consecutive wins of 'Snakes and Ladders', Ali never grew tired of seeing the joy on his daughter's face. He'd spend the whole night playing board games with his children if he could, but he knew each of them needed to be well-rested for the morning.

Taking his son into his lap, Ali guided Sami's hand to allow him to roll the dice. As his token reached the goal, it was time to wrap up the game for the night. Ali patted his daughter on the head as she gloated about her victory and he turned to his wife who walked slowly into the room.

"My mom called," she said, "I think she is right. What is left in Pakistan? You work so hard but your salary is so low. Over in America, we can have good treatment for Sami. Our future is going to get better. We don't even live in the city. We are living in Kashmir. It is dark and lonely and I don't feel comfortable."

Ali was silent as he listened to his wife, "The conditions here aren't nice anymore. The schools are not safe. The food and medicine are not pure. The hospitals don't provide good care and there are robberies. And... from what I have read in the newspaper... my heart pounds in fear that you or Rabia won't come home."

Before she could say another word, there was a knock on the door. Judging by the pattern— two knock, a pause, and three more knocks —she knew exactly who it was. Her breathing and voice became more frantic as she continued to speak.

"And you're in the habit of always helping everyone."

She walked back to the kitchen mumbling to herself as she gathered food onto a plate, "I never see anyone helping you, but you help everyone. With medical bills and our children's schooling, how will we manage when you give so much of your salary away?"

The way she felt was something Ali had known for a long time, but it was only recently that she expressed it in her own words. Seeing her distress, Ali knew what he needed to do. He took the plate and placed it onto the table. With his eyes locked of hers, he smiled at his wife.

"Okay. I understand. I'm ready."

Taking a moment to gaze up at him, Mehwish's petal-like lips grinned. She exclaimed, "You're the best! I love you!"

Ali smiled back at her, but she hid her face shyly behind her hands, "I'm sorry I've spoken so much today."

It was her sweet nature that drew him in most. Mehwish had a gentle heart, but most of all, she worried greatly for her family. And in turn, Ali did not wish to worry her. If there was something he could do for her, he would do it without question.

He touched her shoulder, "It's okay. Don't worry about it."

After hugging his wife, he took the plate and went to the door. Moving away from Kashmir meant that there would be many that he would need to leave behind. And because of all that he gave, there were many who depended on Ali for help. But he knew that there were those in need everywhere in the world.

Outside of his home sat an old man with a cigarette in his mouth. As Ali approached him, he shook his head and plucked the cigarette away. In its place, Ali offered the man a plate of food instead. What he needed was to regain his strength and smoking would only damage him further.

Ali sat beside the man who began to pray, "You are a nice man, Ali. God will give you everything. You will see one day."

Hearing those words made him smile, "Thank you, sir. How is Hassan? How is your son doing?"

But the old man turned sullen, "As usual, he's left for the mountains."

Raising his head to view the towering trees of the forest, worry-filled Ali's mind. The way the snow fell, he knew it would be unsafe to travel such roads at night. But after what Hassan had said at the tea shop, he knew that nothing would change the man's mind. All he could do any longer was to pray.

SCENE VIII

Back inside his home, Ali returned the emptied plate to the kitchen sink where Mehwish stood washing the countertops. It was nice to see that Hassan's father was eating, but it troubled Ali that he still continued to smoke. And on top of that, Hassan himself continued to chase the Green Darwaish.

Those thoughts were troublesome, but seeing his wife always made him smile. His children had been tucked into bed where they could sleep soundly. And with all in order, he finally had a moment that he could share alone with his dear wife.

He looked at her and his heart pounded as her large green eyes locked with his. He heard voices— the TV was still playing. But he wanted nothing to stand between the two at that moment. After a long day, he wanted to have time to devote to her as well.

But as he placed his hand on her shoulder, the sound of the TV grew louder. As much as Ali wished to drown it out, it was difficult to ignore. And even if he tried to forget about the noise alone, it was what the news anchors were saying that startled him most.

Mehwish paused. She understood her husband's worry. The report was about tensions between Pakistan and India. The bickering had gone back and forth for long enough, but it had escalated to violence. Not wanting to stand and watch their soldiers fall, Pakistan decided to strike back.

Ali's breathing grew thick and his eyes were wide. He said nothing, but to Mehwish, his expression alone explained more than any words could. She reached for the remote to turn off the TV. Her husband did so much for everyone around him. She believed freeing him from what tormented him was something small that she could give back to him.

SCENE IX

As he dreamt, Ali was covered in sweat. Most nights had been getting better. It was rare for him to have so many nightmares any longer. But when something reminded him of the war— whether it was through mention of the past or hinting of the future —he was unable to sleep easily.

The images in his mind were like dark shadows. They were figments that he believed he had seen at some point in time. But now, they were all but lost in his memories. The faces and voices— Ali was uncertain if they were inventions of his dreams or memories that he tried to lock away.

He saw himself at the border. What began as an empty field full of trees and the chirping sound of birds turned to total chaos. Bullets shot past him. Instead of chirping, all he could hear were screams. As he took a step forward, he began to recognize the faces as colleagues. Every soldier he fought alongside was with him.

The stench was putrid. Ali coughed and covered his nose. Flames engulfed the forest and the fallen men around him turned charred. He felt helpless. No matter how he tried to reach out to each soldier, they were taken down by bullets, blades, or fire.

And amongst all of the horrors, he spotted a young boy kneeling on the ground crying. It was as if Ali's heart had stopped beating. He wanted to reach out to the boy and tell him that all would be well. He wanted to rescue him and keep him safe. But in the situation they were in, he couldn't promise anything.

Behind him, a voice screamed, "Kill him… kill him…"

Chest seizing, Ali looked behind but saw only decay. His colleagues had all fallen. And as his eyes wandered, he saw the flames surrounding him from all sides. He rushed to the boy. He wanted to know if he was safe. But before he could move another step, his body froze in place. He was unable to blink or breathe. And he was unable to scream.

Scene X

Jolting awake, Ali checked his surroundings. He was at home in his bed, but after such a fright, his body was drenched in sweat. He needed fresh air and a moment to breathe. The way his heart pounded and beat out of his chest, Ali feared he wouldn't be able to sleep at all.

Quietly, he stepped out to the kitchen to pour himself a glass of water. Gulping down his glass, Ali exhaled. His hands shook as they leaned on the counter. Of all the nightmares he had, that was one of the worst— the vivid details were so frighteningly real, but he knew he had to come to his senses.

"It's just a dream," he whispered to himself.

Ali knew the reality of what happened so many years ago. It was so much more gruesome than he wanted to recall, but he knew it was nothing like the dream. What he dreamt of was fantasy. He tried to reassure himself of that so he could have another chance to fall asleep.

Before he could return to his bedroom, he heard the sound of frantic barking. A wild dog— or perhaps many —were traveling through the cold night. As much as Ali wished to learn the cause of their commotion, his fast-beating heart could take no more.

He tried to talk to himself to ease his mind. It was not uncommon for dogs to run through the nearby forests. With how dense and far the trees stretched back, all sorts of life lurked within. He wanted to tell himself that it was no cause for concern. Ali knew that if he didn't, he truly would get no sleep at all.

SCENE XI

Despite how tired he felt, Ali was at the mosque at the crack of dawn. Hearing the sound of azan breathed life back into him. And after the night he had, it was truly needed. It was hard to shake the panicked feeling out of his chest. As he walked home, the thought of the baby deer was what calmed him and helped him continue forward.

As he reached his barn, he noticed something scurrying through the bushes. The figure was much too large to be a hare. And judging by the way the hooves clopped, Ali had a feeling he knew who exactly had come to check on the new animal in his care.

He held his hand out for the mother deer. She was far too frightened of people to come near, but he knew what would ease her worry. Rushing into the barn, he noticed right away that the young deer was up on his feet, prancing in anticipation. Soon he would be reunited with his mother and Ali was thankful that he allowed such events to occur.

Removing the bandage, Ali gave the baby deer one last check before he swung the stall door opened and allowed the animal to run towards his mother. Still, the older deer was skittish. With the way Ali had found her child, it was no wonder that she would fear humans. But he wanted to give her faith.

The baby deer's legs were still weak despite his eagerness. Ali carried him as he struggled to stand on his own four legs. Seeing the man once more, the mother deer backed away, awaiting what he may do. Hearing her frantic cries, he wished to allow the two to get back together soon.

Helping the young animal to his feet, Ali backed away and watched as the mother caressed her child. As the little deer limped and fell to the ground, the mother was there to nudge him back to his feet and help him return with her into the forest. After a short struggle, the two disappeared out of sight into the dense trees.

It was mesmerising for Ali to watch how delicate life could be. Had he not found the young deer by the road, he feared what outcome may have occurred. And the thought of the two being unable to frolic through the forests saddened him. He wanted all life to live to its fullest.

But as he watched the sweet moment, a strained whinny caught his attention. The hoofsteps he heard this time were far larger and quicker than that of any deer.

His heart pounded as he rushed back inside the barn. He feared something had happened to his horse.

Seeking the source of the kicking hooves and frantic neighs, Ali ran to Tiger and placed a hand on the animal's back. He checked the floor of the barn, worrying that a snake had made its way inside and was planning to attack. But as he sifted through the hay with a long stick, he found nothing.

"Calm down, Tiger," he said, "There's nothing here that will harm you."

Despite his words, the horse continued to thrash and rip his muzzle away from the rope. Seeing the fibers breaking, Ali attempted to hold onto Tiger to keep him from escaping the pen, but it was to no avail. The horse snapped the rope before he could reach him and Tiger was barreling out of the barn towards the forest.

Ali chased after his beloved horse and called his name, but what he received in return was no answer. His own speed couldn't match that of the trained stallion. He watched as his horse disappeared behind a veil of trees. His heart sank as he feared Tiger was injured.

But his eyes turned to the rising sun in the sky. Rabia needed to go to school. And he himself needed to leave for work. In all of his years at the factory, he had never shown up late. Even if it were for his horse, he couldn't risk anything happening to his family and his job.

He shook his head, *"He will come back. He knows his way home. Something only scared him. All will be well."*

SCENE XII

The worry on Ali's face was evident as he stepped through the front door of his home. Mehwish paused as she stood in the kitchen doorway. She knew her husband's heart was too large for even himself to contain. For him to have such a sullen expression, she knew something wasn't right.

But he said nothing. He pushed forward just as if it were any other moment. As Rabia finished eating her breakfast, the two set off for the door to catch the bus. Mehwish respected that Ali gave so much for his family, but she feared that he was sacrificing pieces of himself in the process.

Ali, too, knew that it weighed on his mind that Tiger was lost in the cold. His heart was pounding with guilt but seeing Rabia's smiling face as she greeted the neighbors, he couldn't bear to bring his family into the same state of worry. That was a burden he wished to carry himself.

A loud bark startled Ali from his thoughts. The neighbors were approaching but along with them came their tiny dog Tommy— a ball of fluff and energy. He smiled as he saw the group. He knew that Rabia often liked to play with the dog when she visited her friend. But from the way Tommy snarled his teeth, he knew that something was amiss.

"Tommy!" Hiba cried, "What's wrong!?"

Rushing to the girl's side, he backed her away from Tommy who hung low to the ground as if he meant to attack. His perky ears flattened back against his head and the hairs on his tail stood up like he was a balloon about to burst. In all the years that his neighbor had their small dog, he had never behaved so violently.

"I don't know what's happened," Fariha cried, "He's never done this before. Ali, is he sick?"

There was no foam in the dog's mouth from what Ali could tell. But he couldn't rule out the possibility of rabies. And if that were the case, he had to think of the lives of those around him. He instructed each of them to stay back and avoid the dog that snarled and snapped at them.

It was as if a lightswitch had gone off in the dog's mind. And just like Ali's beloved horse, the dog sprinted to the forest where he was lost out of sight. The coincidence was too large to dismiss. Two animals both behaving so erratically was something Ali wished to fully understand. He had to worry that such events would continue.

Though, turning to Hiba and Fariha, he saw the fear in their eyes. He couldn't tell them about Tiger. He knew it would only worry them further and the school bus was ready to leave. He turned to them and smiled. He wanted to assure them that all would be well and safe.

"It may have been a sound that frightened Tommy. Perhaps a whistle or something. He's a good dog. He'll return. I'm certain of it."

Those words did little to comfort Hiba who worried about her little dog. But Rabia, too, assured her that everything would be well. Ali knew his neighbors trusted him. But he feared diminishing that trust. The moment he was home from work, he was determined to search the entire forest if he had to in search of the missing pets.

There was no reason for panic. In the case of both Tiger and Tommy, they had run through the forests before. They knew their ways back home. He wanted to believe that they would calm down and return to their families.

Ali waved to the girls as they sat on the school bus and he returned to his SUV. While usually a focused driver, Ali couldn't help but stare into the thick forest of trees on his journey to work. Something wasn't right and until he knew what it was, there was no way to rest easily.

In the parking lot of the factory, Ali breathed in deeply. *"All is well. Everything will work out,"* he told himself. But the moment he opened his car door, a large rumbling sound overwhelmed his eardrums. Ali held his gloves against the sides of his head as he peered into the sky. He gulped.

Above, two fighter jets zipped through the sky on their way towards the Indian border. By that pound, his heart was pounding. He needed water to calm himself down and ease his mind. Something was far from well. And as Ali entered the factory, his thoughts were overwhelmed figuring out what it could be.

SCENE XIII

Shards of glass crunched under the weight of the recycling belt's crusher. Even with so many thoughts weighing on his mind, he found solace in his work. At the factory, he knew he could make a difference; he knew there were those who depended on him. And even with so much going wrong at home, he still had a chance to keep everything at the factory running smoothly and safely.

Though, from where he stood from his office looking down at the workshop floor, it seemed the day of unfortunate events was far from over. Pacing back and forth, a worker was seemingly confused about his daily schedule. And that same confusion was shared by his eyes— one was fixated on the wall while another gazed up at the ceiling.

Pressing his face against the office window, Ali tried to get a better look. He knew the worker had to be an employee who joined the company recently. But despite his attempts to get a better view of the man's face, between the worker's erratic movements and the clothing he wore, it was difficult to discern.

Instead of wearing the uniform that was common for the rest of the staff, the man had his half-buttoned shirt worn backward. A jarring orange jacket clashed against the light blue button-up and his hardhat was covered in what appeared to be spray paint. Between that and the dirt-stained pants and untied shoelaces, Ali knew that the man wasn't in his right mind.

Ali winced as the man approached a pillar. It was a wide sheet of metal— clearly solid to any with sight. But the peculiar man banged into it as if he were walking through air. The wall, not having the capacity to change out of a solid-state, stopped the man in his tracks and sent him falling back on his rear.

As guilty as he felt for watching such a spectacle, Ali had to wonder what was going on with the strange worker. The man flailed on his back like a turtle wobbling on his shell. Such behavior was far from lucid and Ali had to wonder if, among the new employees, one had taken to drugs.

Jumping back on his feet, the man grew more frantic. Leaving the conveyor belt, his sights were set on a wall of hanging cables which he rushed to like a child wanting candy. Tripping once more, the worker found himself tangled and trapped in the cables. And that's when Ali realized he had to step in.

By the time Ali reached the factory floor, the worker was placing frayed wires to his tongue, zapping himself with a small jolt. It seemed amusing to the man to light the bulbs by his own hands. Ali, though, wasn't laughing at the man's antics. He wanted to know the meaning of such unstable behaviour.

The closer Ali got to the man, the clues began to fall into place. The round brown eyes and thin beard— it was the worker he had lent rupees to help with his sick mother. Anger overwhelmed Ali as he realized that he had been tricked. The worker, Saleem, had a far more nefarious use for the advance in pay.

Standing before the man, Ali saw the worker's eyes grow wide. "Oh, shit!" he exclaimed before he ran towards the loading bay. How he expected to make it through an entire workday without being seen was a mystery to Ali. But when dealing with someone who wasn't in a clear state of mind, anything was possible.

Ali ran after the man. He refused to let him get away with lying, stealing money for drugs, and endangering his fellow workers. Though, the wild chase was cut short the moment Saleem reached the cold, icy roads. Just one misstep caught him off-balance and he was left scrambling and spinning while his trousers fell to his knees.

Underwear exposed, Saleem attempted to free himself from his snowy prison. His movements appeared as if he was scuba diving above land. While unable to break himself free, he certainly continued to make a spectacle of himself. And Ali wished to bring that show to an end.

"What the- What do you think you're doing, Saleem!?"

It was uncommon for Ali to raise his voice, but at that moment, he was overcome by rage. Never did he suspect that the young man whom he offered money and support would betray his trust in favor of drugs. He wanted to figure out what was going on.

SCENE XIV

The look on Saleem's face was a mix of shame, fear, and worry. At least, that was the sense Ali felt as he looked down at him. With his bloodshot eyes and itchy, inflamed skin, it was hard to discern what was remorse and what was a side-effect of the drugs.

From the cold, Ali dragged Saleem into one of the work sheds. As much as he believed he deserved the fate of being trapped in the snow, Ali needed to talk and understand Saleem's state of mind. If he was still coherent, he wished to know the cause for such erratic behavior.

Ali sighed, "Why?"

"I… okay. I'm an addict," Saleem, "I have to do it. You don't even want to see me when I don't. It's… it's a mess. I'm sorry I lied to you. But… I have no parents.

This job is all I have and if I didn't get the money soon enough-"

"Shut up," Ali said as he groaned, "You chose to take drugs. And you chose to lie. Tell me. How long have you been doing this? And how many people have you been tricking with your false stories?"

Saleem shook his head, "Seriously! I'm telling the truth. I don't lie. Well, not usually. I know you're so kind and I knew you would help me if I asked. I have no mother or father. I have no one! I had nowhere else to turn."

Just as Saleem finished speaking, a fellow worker peeked his head into the shed. Oblivious to the conversation that was occurring, he whistled to himself while handing a file to Ali. Upon seeing Saleem, he greeted him with a friendly wave. Though, Saleem gulped audibly.

"How's your father? Is he getting treatment?" the man asked.

Ali stared daggers at Saleem who wove yet another tale. Whatever was the truth, Ali didn't expect to learn it from the young worker. With a swift nod, Saleem's colleague bid him farewell. There were only Ali and the young worker left in the room with an awkward silence between them.

Saleem stammered, "Wait. Wait! I can explain. It was-"

But Ali wished to hear none of it, "Let me tell you a story. I know about those with drug addictions. I lost two of my childhood friends to drugs."

As Ali continued, Saleem remained silent, "Everything was fine. They were good people with so much love and life. But once they started abusing drugs, they turned to darkness. They had always been competitive with each other. They competed in sports, to get better jobs… and eventually, they both came to love the same girl."

"They became so aggressive," Ali said with a strained voice, "When I got the call that there was a fight between them, I didn't want to believe it, but my heart knew it was true. By the end of that night, I learned that one of my friends was dead. And the other soon went to jail. In that one night, the lives of two families were ruined."

Moving closer to Saleem, Ali gripped him by his collar, "And that's why I hate drugs. I hate what it does to people. They turn violent. They lie. They-"

Before Ali could say another word, he was startled by the sound coming from the shed's TV. The chime of 'Breaking News' was one he was used to hearing. Between the robberies and violent crimes, there was no shortage of reasons to warn the public. But it was the words the news anchors said that caused him to panic.

"The war has begun in Kashmir."

It had to be a mistake. Ali couldn't believe what he was hearing. He whipped his head around, hoping that he had been mistaken. But the images on the screen showed the horrible truth that he hoped to avoid. The army was mobilizing. Tanks and jeeps were stationed at every border and checkpoint. And the jets he heard overhead—he could now confirm what they truly were.

Saleem shouted, "Oh shit! A war!? We're at war!? It's started!? Is India coming!? What's going on!?"

Ali pulled Saleem's arm as he rushed back inside to his office. His heart was racing but he knew he needed to stay calm. The safety of every worker was on his mind. And he knew he needed to get back to his family as soon as possible. Whatever would happen, Ali believed he would do anything to keep his family safe.

Removing a phone from the wall, Ali's calm voice echoed over the loudspeaker, "We are evacuating the factory. There is no need for panic. We are going to form a single-file line and exit the factory. Shut down any machinery, return to your vehicles, and reach your families immediately. If you can, call your wives and children. We need to leave Kashmir."

On the wall, Ali uncovered a large red button from a glass case and pressed it. Lights flashed and a siren roared. Every machine and conveyor belt powered down. And as Ali looked down from his office window, he saw the workers silently exiting the building. He was relieved but still worried. The reality of what was happening hadn't fully hit him. He couldn't believe another war had begun.

SCENE XV

It felt like his greatest nightmare had come true. The peaceful life that he had always promised his family had been threatened. Running to his SUV, he wanted to hope that panic hadn't sent his neighborhood into an uproar. He needed to hear Mehwish's voice. He wanted to know that she was safe.

Taking his phone in hand, Ali called his wife. He knew she had to have heard the news already— he assumed every TV and radio station in Kashmir was filled with the news. But he wanted to speak with Mehwish directly in hopes that they could coordinate a plan out of the city.

Hearing static on his cellphone's receiver, Ali's heart sank. He checked his phone and saw that there was no signal available. No calls or messages could go through. His eyes watched the sky. He feared that the signals were being jammed. *"Are we already under attack?"*

He ran from the parking lot back into the factory. There was a chance that the landlines were still working. And if that were the case, he needed to have another chance to hear from his family and know they weren't caught up in any danger. He felt sweat building on his palms by the time he reached his office.

The receiver slipped from Ali's hands as he dialed his wife's number. Hearing the ringing sound alleviated some of his worries, but it wasn't until he heard his wife's voice that he was able to breathe easily. She was frantic when she picked up the phone, but Ali knew he needed to stay calm to ease her mind.

"Everything will be okay," Ali said, "I'll pick up Rabia from school. I need you to pack up everything we'll need— food, clothing, water... as soon as I'm home, we'll leave Kashmir together."

She was holding back tears. Ali could tell by the way her voice was strained. He knew she had to be frightened. He, too, was frightened. But he trusted she was strong. He knew she would be able to handle everything back at home. But Ali still feared what was happening at Rabia's school.

Seeing the dark and empty factory spelled out the situation everyone faced. The normal life that everyone knew was over. Darkness had swept over the city of Kashmir and there was no telling when, or even if, everything would be the same again.

The moment Ali entered his vehicle, he shifted gears and sped out of the empty lot. Seeing not one car left helped ease his thoughts of anyone being left behind. And when he got on the main road, it was deserted save for piles of snow and withered branches. For that reason, though, Ali felt uneasy.

There was complete silence. On his car's radio, there was only static. Whether the stations themselves were off the air or if it was caused by something else, Ali couldn't be certain. As each snowflake fell, he believed his eyes were playing tricks on him— he was seeing images out of the corner of his eye.

Ali shook his head. He knew his state of mind left him with racing thoughts. But he had to assure himself that there was no danger. *"We still have time. We can still make it to the city."* He looked into his rear-view mirror. There was a shadow behind him. As much as Ali wanted to assume it was a fallen branch, the ominous sight came from inside the car.

In a panic, Ali slammed on his breaks and skidded onto the side of the road. It was unmistakable. He saw something move in his back seat. He knew his car was empty earlier. There was nothing that could have fallen. Trying to remain logical, he tried to think of a cause, but his mind was blank. All he could think of was fleeing from whatever was inside his car.

As his feet crunched into the snow, Ali tried to collect himself. *"What am I doing!? I need to get to Rabia!"* Whatever it was that he saw, Ali knew that it couldn't stand in the way of him protecting his family. He slowly stepped his way towards the back seat window, trying to peek at what was hidden inside.

Growing closer, he saw a darkened silhouette. Two legs and two arms— it was a person that was inside his SUV. Under other circumstances, he would be frightened. But noticing the clothing of the person in question, Ali put two and two together of who it was.

"Saleem!? What are you *doing*!? Come. Get in the front seat."

The young worker was quiet as he complied with the orders. The situation wasn't ideal, but Ali refused to leave anyone behind given everything that was happening. He may have been a liar, but no one deserved to be alone and scared. Ali sped away, hoping that everyone in his neighborhood would be safe.

SCENE XVI

In the empty factory parking lot, a single silver sedan sped towards the front doors of the offices. The driver exited the vehicle, brushing his long hair out of his face. His purple eyes were bulging as he pounded on the door, calling out for someone to answer. Hassan desperately sought his friend.

Without a key to enter the factory, he was left banging on the glass, peering inside the windows, and checking the sheds in the back. When he spotted the loading bay at been left open, Hassan rushed inside and called out Ali's name. But despite a lingering echo, he was met with silence.

The interior of the factory was dark. The machines had stopped working and even as he had witnessed from the parking lot outside, no one was left in the factory. While part of him was relieved, another part of him was fearful of the uncertainty. He had no way of knowing what became of his dear friend.

Hassan sped back to his car, skidding on ice. *"I have to reach him... I have to reach him before..."* He pressed his key into the ignition and sped off onto the road. There was so much he wished he had said to Ali sooner. And given the circumstances, he feared he would never be able to.

SCENE XVII

While the roads leaving the factory were deserted, the closer Ali drove to the center of town, the more he found chaos. Not only were the streets littered with cars but civilians took to the shops. In a last-ditch effort to gather as much food and supplies as they could before leaving the city, people stampeded to and from the parking lots.

And by the time Ali reached Rabia's school, he quickly learned there was no end to the panic. As he rushed from his SUV, he saw the walkway leading up to the school littered with books, articles of clothing, and school supplies. Backpacks and coats were tossed as parents shuffled their children into their vehicles. The only priority was returning home as soon as possible.

If the mess wasn't enough, the sounds, too, alerted Ali. Screams came from the crowds. Parents searched desperately for their children. But within the frantic hoards, spotting anyone was difficult. Ali was saddened to see adults and children alike teary-eyed and frightened.

But even bombarded by so many sounds, Ali recognized the voice of his daughter. Rabia called out to him and he rushed to her. She and her friend Hiba were huddled together, avoiding get swept up with the crowd. While thankful to see both his daughter and the neighbor safe, a thought crossed his mind.

"Hiba," he said, "Where is your mother?"

The young girl wept. As Ali searched through the crowd, he saw no sight of Fariha. Calling out her name did nothing; Ali's voice couldn't cut through the shrieks and screams. He knew he couldn't wait for too long, but he also knew that he couldn't leave Hiba stranded.

"She doesn't have a car!" Rabia cried, "Hiba's mother can't come to pick her up."

Ali had to make a judgment call and he decided to take Hiba with them. He could only hope that Fariha was still at home, packing her bags. It was not long ago that he spoke to Mehwish. He had to believe that she had contacted Fariha and the two were coordinating their plans to leave Kashmir.

Piling everyone into the car— Ali and Saleem in the front and Hiba and Rabia in the back —the four returned to the road. Dodging other vehicles was a challenge in itself. Fearful drivers worrying for their lives were colliding with each other and blocking off the roads.

Pulling his tires onto the curb, Ali managed to weave around the broken-down cars. But he soon learned that was far from the end of his worries. From the sky, Ali heard a metallic roar. Peering above, he saw the flames— a fighter plane was spinning towards a field. Ali screamed for the children to cover their eyes and ears as the plane crashed.

B-O-O-M.

Clutching his hands tightly against his wheel, Ali tried to keep his SUV steady. The impact of the crashing plane sent a shockwave onto the road. He saw other cars crash and meander onto the curbs and away from the field. Making it home in one piece was going to be a struggle, but Ali was determined.

"Oh shit!" Saleem screamed, "Did you see that!? Shit! We're *doomed*!"

Removing one hand from the wheel, Ali covered Saleem's mouth and reminded him that children were in the back seat. It was true that the situation was grim. And he, too, was frightened. But he had to remain strong for Rabia and Hiba. He wanted to show them that everything was going to be alright.

There was no end to the destruction as they drove. Planes, tanks, and cars all burned and were left broken down by the roadside. Ali had never seen so much of an uproar since the war… and that's when it truly sunk in. The peace he and his family had long enjoyed was finally over.

Ali's eyes grew wide and he slammed on his breaks. What he saw before him was no man or machine. And the fact that he couldn't comprehend what he was looking at was what alarmed him most of all. Saleem, too, was overwhelmed by chills. Saleem's teeth chattered so loud, Ali feared they would shatter.

In front of the car stood a pack of what seemed to be a thousand dogs. Their numbers were so tightly packed and spread so far that Ali was unable to see the road beyond them. And it wasn't only the sheer amount but their appearance that was menacing. Their eyes were red and bloodshot. And bucketfuls of drool spilled from their mouths.

"What the fuck!? This can't be real!" Saleem slapped himself, "That's it. I'm not doing drugs anymore. I'm dreaming, right!? I'm just high, right!? This isn't real!? Ali! Is this-"

Ali slapped Saleem across the face, silencing him. The situation in itself was a nightmare. He didn't need to deal with a second fiend frightening his children. Looking into the back seat, the two girls were huddled close, closing their eyes and ears and blocking out the world around them.

"Your hand is like an iron rod. Man. How do you hit so-"

"Shut up! Just stay quiet!" Ali screamed to Saleem.

Examining the dogs, Ali spoke once more, "I... I don't think they can see us. They're worried."

Though vicious in appearance, the dogs remained still. Their reddened eyes were searching for something but it was as if they were looking through the car itself. Many possibilities entered Ali's mind. He wondered if a chemical attack had left the animals rabid. It was difficult for him to understand what else could have caused so many dogs to gather together.

Another roar came from the sky. This time, a plane was crashing down into the forest. As the plane's burning wings touched the pines, they were set ablaze. Ali's heart sank. That very forest led to his home. It was the place where he'd feed wild animals that'd visit his barn. And it was the last place he saw his beloved horse.

As the plane crashed, the dogs were alerted. They cocked their heads as if broken and ran to the trees. Ali felt sick to his stomach. It was hard to believe that anything was reality, but he finally had a chance to flee. With the road cleared, Ali slammed on his gas pedal and traveled home.

SCENE XVIII

The tires of Ali's car screeched as he pulled into the driveway. Rust or worn rubber of consequence to him. The only thought on Ali's mind was gathering his family and getting everyone out of Kashmir as quickly as possible.

He yelled to everyone in the car to exit. Before they could go anywhere, they first needed to be packed and ready. And Ali had another dilemma on his hands. Hiba was still with them. Despite his hopes that Fariha would be home, there was no sight of her anywhere.

"Fariha's probably inside. She couldn't have gone far," Ali thought to himself.

Hearing the car doors close, Mehwish rushed outside. In her arms, she held Sami. Her eyes motioned towards the doorway. There were four large suitcases packed. Ali rushed for the bags and drug them towards the SUV. The two girls, though frightened, ran alongside him to help. It was only Saleem who stayed behind, holding his head in his hands.

"Hiba!" Ali called out, "I'll run next door to your mother. Stay here."

Before sending the young girl off on her own, he needed to be certain that all was well and safe. After seeing what had happened to the wild dogs, he wondered what else was lurking in the forests. Though, before he could make it past his fence, his wife called out to him.

"What are you doing!? Fariha went to the school. She went to pick up Hiba!"

Luggage spilled onto the ground. Both Ali and Mehwish's eyes grew wide. It dawned on both of them that the mother and daughter were split up with no way of contacting each other. There was no way of calling Fariha to let her know that Hiba was safe. Ali felt an emptiness in the back of his throat as he imagined the despairing thoughts on the mother's mind.

There wasn't time to drive back to search for Fariha. And more importantly, it wasn't *safe*. The journey to his home alone had been a treacherous one. The journey to the city would only be more challenging. But Ali couldn't fathom leaving his neighbor stranded in Kashmir.

"Quick!" Saleem screamed, "Quick! Let's go! Let's go to Islamabad! Why are we stalling!?"

Mehwish tilted her head at the strange man with bloodshot eyes. Ali was already regretting bringing the young factory worker with him, but he couldn't leave a man stranded on the road during a time of war. Though, he had to worry that Saleem would endanger his family.

Ali stormed towards the man who had fumbled onto the ground and flailed in the snow. His heart was pounding. After everything that had happened, he couldn't risk anything happening to the people he loved. He needed to calm Saleem. He needed him to listen to reason.

But as Ali stood in front of the young worker, he heard a loud screech. Tires slid into his driveway. At first, he feared a car had been run off the road or an accident had occurred. But as he looked into the window and saw a man with long hair and purple eyes, he sighed with relief.

Hassan exited his vehicle, but he was not alone. A woman got out of the car with him. When Ali saw her, he gasped. Hiba screamed and ran towards her mother. The two, finally, had been reunited. Ali was thankful to his friend. He wasn't certain what he would have done otherwise.

Though, while the mother and daughter enjoyed their reunion, there was still confusion on Ali's mind. *"How did Hassan find her? Why did he come here? Shouldn't he and his father be fleeing Kashmir?"* He stepped forward to greet his friend. Time was limited, but he needed answers.

"I am thankful," Ali said, "But how? Where did you find Fariha?"

"I went to your work to look for you. When I didn't find you there, I figured you had gone to pick up your daughter. Fariha was worried, but I knew if you found both of the children, they would be with you."

Ali was growing anxious, "We need to leave Kashmir! Get in your car. We need to go now!"

Hassan was calm, "There is no use."

Those words took Ali by surprise. He never knew Hassan to be one for such pessimism. There was still a chance. Ali refused to accept that there was no hope. He would stop at nothing to keep everyone safe. If they could just get to the city then-

"They are everywhere," Hassan continued, "And I don't mean just in Islamabad. They are attacking London, New York, Tokyo, Hong Kong... they're attacking the entire world."

"But..." Ali was shocked, "What? The war is here in Kashmir!"

Hassan pointed inside the house, "Have you not been watching? This is not between Pakistan and India."

All eyes were on Hassan. Ever since he had left the office, he hadn't checked the news— he couldn't. The radio in his car wasn't working. And among the chaos, he hadn't had a moment to stop. He looked at Mehwish who gasped. She, too, didn't know what Hassan meant.

"Everyone! Get inside the house. I will explain everything!" Hassan said.

SCENE XIX

Hassan held out his cellphone and played the clip—it was exactly as he described. The destruction that Ali had witnessed was not only isolated in his hometown. In New York, skyscrapers burned. In Singapore, civilians dove into the waters to avoid the onslaught of crashing vehicles. And in Sydney, planes collided in the sky sending shrapnel into the streets below.

Ali was at a loss for words. What he witnessed was something he never believed could be possible. It was horrifying enough to imagine that war had come to Kashmir. But that it was worldwide? Ali felt sweat forming at the back of his neck. He was uncertain of what to do or where to take his family.

But there was still the burning question: *who?* Who was responsible for the attacks? He couldn't believe that any one country could be responsible for the devastation. After all, the entire world was affected. Judging by the amount of damage as well, something truly sinister was at play.

Before Ali had a chance to ask Hassan how he was able to get a signal, Mehwish rushed for the TV. She needed to confirm that the images online were truthful. She didn't want to believe that the entire world was in ruins. She wanted to hope it was all a sick joke.

When she turned on the TV, however, everyone was shocked by the headline— Alien Invasion.

It was as if the room was spinning. No one wanted to believe their ears or eyes. It seemed so impossible. But the evidence was too great to deny. The images from Hassan's cellphone were playing again on the TV. This time, there was even more footage and even more cities being destroyed.

Amsterdam was on fire. The landmarks of Paris were obliterated into fragments. And Seoul had almost all been leveled. Nowhere was safe. As Ali looked at his family, he held them tightly. It was as Hassan said. It truly was of no use. Islamabad was in just as much turmoil as anywhere else.

On the news, the general of Pakistan's army stood at a podium. His microphone cut in and out as he spoke, but one could truly hear the hopelessness in his voice. He was deadpan. His tone may have remained calm, but there was hesitation. He needed to remain strong. Though, it was unknown whether strength alone would be enough.

"From what we've gathered, this is a highly intelligent race. They've planned this down to the very second. They knew where our militaries were stationed. Not just here in Pakistan— they knew how to locate all of humanity's armies. And they triggered our weapons against each other."

Hearing that, it all began to make sense to Ali. There had been so much tension with India and he didn't understand. After the war had passed, he had hoped that his home could finally remain at peace. Though, he certainly didn't guess that *aliens* would have been the cause.

The general continued, "We thought India was attacking. We were mobilizing and preparing ourselves for a counter-attack... and that's when we were caught off-guard. All of our weapon systems were hijacked. And we know it wasn't only us. All units and all weapons everywhere in the world— they've all been taken over."

"So now..." the TV anchor was teary-eyed, "Do you think we're all alone? We have no help? No hope? No defense? The aliens... who are they and what do they want?"

"If I had any guess it's that their only purpose is to destroy humanity. This is a complete take-over. We have no idea how many there are, but they have the capability to hijack all of our machinery. Entire hospitals are under their control. We have people without food, water, and shelter..."

The anchor was quiet, "By this rate… we'll be finished. What… what is the military's plan?"

Averting his eyes, the general said, "Accept God. We have no one to help us. We have no backup plans. Stay inside your homes. Stay silent. Ration all food and avoid traveling."

What Ali heard was hard to swallow. Even the general of their army was of the mindset that all was lost. *"No. It can't be real. There has to be something. There has to be a way."* Looking at the faces of his friends and family, everyone was overwhelmed by shock and grief.

Fariha's lip trembled. Ali tried to comfort her before she screamed, "Where's Hiba!?"

The adults shot up to their feet. They had been mesmerized by the news for so long that they didn't realize that one of the children had fled. Immediately, Ali rushed to the window in hopes of spotting the young girl before she had gone too far. He was able to see her… but he also saw something far more menacing.

Hiba stood in the middle of the road reaching her arms out towards a tiny dog. Though far more disheveled with tattered fur and bloodshot eyes, Ali recognized the dog as Tommy. He, like the dogs from the road earlier, had a deadened gaze on his face and drool spilling off of his loose tongue.

Seeing the small dog rear up as if he were ready to lunge, Ali rushed outside. Hassan followed alongside him, shouting it hopes that the dog would flee and leave

Hiba alone. To Ali's surprise, Saleem came barreling behind them. His movements were erratic as always, but Ali hoped that, too, would convince Tommy to run.

Swooping down from the sky, a hawk reached his talons towards Tommy. Hiba gasped and dove away as the bird flew between them. Frightened by Tommy's snarling growl, the hawk flapped his wings and flew off towards the towering trees of the forest. The dog followed the bird inside the dark brush. And young Hiba chased after her dear family pet.

"Hiba! Wait!" Ali called. But it was too late.

The young girl was already lost inside the forest. There was no choice. The three men followed after her, worrying about what dangers lurked in the darkness. If a pack of what appeared to be a thousand dogs were running loose in Kashmir, Ali didn't want any of them to be caught up in the wrong part of town.

Hiba, though, was only frightened for her dog. She couldn't understand all that was happening. All she knew that was Tommy was unwell and she wanted to help him. But what she found in the forest wasn't only Tommy. She spotted a pack of five angry dogs snarling and dripping blood from their mouths.

It was the hawk's last day taking flight. The rabid dogs tore the animal feather from bone. Little remained by the time each of them sank in their fangs. And Hiba was frightened.

As the young girl watched the gruesome scene, she felt something wrap around her cheek. She wished to squeal, but she felt something covering her mouth. Gripping on it, she felt warm skin and five digits— a hand. Hiba was relieved as she looked up and saw Ali.

Motioning for her to remain silent, the two slowly backed away from the dogs. Behind him, Ali noticed Hassan and Saleem running through the forest. Ali raised his hand and motioned for both of them to be silent. Hassan got the message right away and slowed his pace. But Saleem continued to barrel forward.

Lunging for the young worker, Ali grabbed him by the collar and pointed towards the dogs. The sight of five sets of bloodstained teeth was all it took for the man's skin to turn yellow and for him to halt in his tracks. They were all gathered, but they needed to leave.

Signally to everyone, Ali led the way for everyone to exit the forest. They were lucky to go unnoticed by the dogs. Fixated on their prey, the dogs paid no mind to the four as they slowly backed out of the forest. Ali's beating heart calmed. It seemed that finally, everything would work itself out. And then he heard the sound.

Click.

Ali looked down. During his days in the army, he had become all too familiar with the short cylindrical object. He knew the dangers of setting foot on undeveloped land. And he remembered how he would always tell his friends and family to look down as they took a step. But in a panic, he failed to heed his own advice and he had stepped on a landmine.

Time was limited. Ali knew that the moment he released his foot, the mine would explode. He remained silent and still. Ali knew what would happen. He knew it was too late to save himself. But at the very least, he hoped he'd be able to save Hiba and his friends.

Ali made eye contact with Hassan. Seeing his friend's calm yet foreboding face, the long-haired man was startled. He looked down and spotted the cause for such a blank-eyed stare— the mine. Hassan, too, knew what fate was inevitable.

Hassan tried to approach Ali. As much as he knew what was about to unfold, he refused to accept the death of his best friend. But the moment he attempted to run towards Ali, the calm man raised a hand forward. He knew what it meant: Stop.

In a soft voice, Ali spoke, "I love my wife and kids. I love them more than anything. Hassan. You must take care of them. Help them reach their grandparents in America. There has to be somewhere that's still safe."

Ali handed Hiba off to Hassan and the two men nodded. Neither wanted such events to be true, but they knew what had to be done in the situation. As Hassan carried Hiba away, she sobbed. And that was the final sound that alerted the rabid dogs. They spotted the group and rushed after them.

"Hassan! Run!" Ali screamed.

Saleem stumbled through the trees, trying to keep up as Hassan lead the way out of the forest. But even as his sole focus was on keeping the young child safe, he couldn't help but turn his head back to view the scene taking place. He wanted to believe there was still hope for his friend.

The five dogs lunged for Ali. Their fangs were barred and their clawed paws outstretched. But instead of fear on his face, Ali had found peace. The thought of death left him with emptiness. But he knew that he was allowing his dear friends to escape. If he could have any death, it was his hope that it would save the lives of others.

Ali released his foot from the mine. The spark he saw was the very last light before he closed his eyes. As the dogs lunged for him, they were blown away by a terrible force. They whimpered and wailed as the explosion shot them into the air and sent them into the bushes and trees.

Hassan couldn't breathe. His chest was seizing. As much as he wished to continue on, he couldn't keep running without knowing the state of his dear friend. The outcome was inevitable. But Hassan couldn't accept it as truth. He couldn't let the man who saved his own life die right in front of him.

Handing Hiba off to Saleem, Hassan returned to the source of the blast. He released a quiet wail as he saw him— Ali was lying on the ground charred. The image was burned into his mind. It pained him for his last memory of his friend to be in such a gruesome death.

But before Hassan turned, he saw movement. Ali, against all odds, raised one arm in the air. He was far from well. His skin was bleeding and burned. And it appeared as if his other limbs were broken by the way they jutted out of place. But still, the man tried to carry on.

It was at that moment that Hassan froze. In his mind, there was a chance. This was a sign. If Ali was still alive, it meant that God was watching over him. That was the only way Hassan could fathom how Ali was able to survive such a devastating blow.

He ran to his friend and scooped him onto his shoulders. Ali, against all odds, had lived. Hassan believed that he had a second chance to protect his best friend. And he intended to do everything in his power to make that a reality.

SCENE XX

A sluggish groan escaped from the lips of blonde woman, Anna, who sat at the head of the boardroom table, "They've destroyed all of our major defense systems. Weapons, satellites— we have nothing to fall back on. And it seems like the local wildlife has also been affected. Though, we are still performing tests to confirm why these animals are affected."

At the table, members from every branch of Geneva's United Nations office crammed together to get a glimpse of the screen before them. Teams from the Telecommunications, Human Rights, and Peace committees sat awaiting what they hoped would be a solution to what seemed like the inevitable destruction of everything.

What Anna, the lead scientist from Stockholm's environmental research branch, pulled up on the screen, however, was something that drained their remaining shreds of hope. For the first time, they caught a glimpse of the aliens. At least, it was what they presumed to be aliens. The 'beings' they saw were robotic in nature and far beyond what anyone expected.

A slender metallic capsule with a smooth triangular 'head'. Propellers kept them hovering mid-air and their small size allowed them the agility to deflect and avoid on-coming fire. That was if one even had time to land an attack on one of the drones.

Their numbers far exceeded what the scientists believed to be possible. For beings that had seemingly arrived out of nowhere, there were thousands stationed strategically throughout the world. It was clear to everyone that this attack had been in the making for quite some time.

Along with the scientist and humanitarian teams were generals who hoped to learn more about the invasion to launch a counter-assault. But even their minds were full of doubt as they watched the images. Humanity was ill-prepared for what they were facing.

Videos depicted soldiers pointing their guns at the drones. But before they had a chance to pull the trigger, they were disintegrated by the drone's laser. The same went for tanks and planes. Even aiming at one of the drones was enough for the aliens to send missiles in retaliation.

"From what we've been able to determine," Anna said, "The only bases that have been able to remain active are those with no military involvement. The aliens are able to track weapons. We've seen this in the US, Russia, China… they've first increased tensions and pitted rival nations against each other. Now they've come to wipe out the rest."

War had always been a constant. There were no members of the UN who could truly say that humanity was ever getting closer to a time of lasting peace. Different nations, factions, and races— humanity always had a reason to wage war and attempt to destroy each other.

But there was now a common threat. No matter where one lived, the aliens were the main fear in everyone's mind. Entire cities were burning, families were separated, and no one truly knew how long it would be until everything was finally over.

"The drones do have a weakness. We've isolated a small fuse-box looking device that knocks them out of service if hit," Anna was sullen, "But hitting them in itself is the issue. Once they spot our weapons and lock on, we've defenseless."

Gasps broke out from the crowd as the screen depicted civilians running through the streets of major cities shooting at the drones only to be gunned down. No one was safe. And no one knew what direction to take to protect themselves and the ones they loved.

A general rose to his feet, "The end of time has begun."

Scene XXI

Running with Ali on his shoulders, the stench of burned flesh made Hassan queasy. It was difficult for him to even look at his dear friend who oozed blood from every section of his body. The fact that Ali was even still breathing was a miracle. And Hassan was determined to save him.

He screamed at Saleem to open his car door, throwing him the keys. Though his mind was full of racing thoughts, Saleem poured all of his focus on preparing the back seat for Ali. The experience was sobering. His mind and body still ached, craving the drug, but he couldn't turn his back on Ali. After everything, he knew he needed to make things right.

"Take Hiba to her mother and then get back here. He doesn't have much time!" Hassan screamed as he guided Ali's body into the sedan.

But before Saleem could take another step, Fariha had come to check on the commotion. And behind her, Mehwish came as well. Seeing her husband's body limp and falling apart, she screamed. Blood dripped from his leg which hung by mere tendons. Her head spun.

"Mehwish!" Fariha screamed as her friend collapsed.

Hassan called out to her, "Please, Fariha. Take care of Mehwish. Everything will be okay. I promise."

"Saleem!" he screamed to the young worker who scurried back and forth like a squirrel, "Get in the car!"

The tires skid and sent snow into the air as Hassan took off down the road. Fariha told the children to wait inside as she cradled Mehwish in her lap. After seeing the state of Ali, she didn't know what to expect. But truthfully, she didn't know if anything mattered at all given the situation. It seemed like nothing could save *anyone*.

Despite the doubts, Hassan was determined. His vehicle bumped and slid down the road as he sped out of the development toward the mountain pass. Speed breakers and stop signs meant little to him as he barreled and wove past everything in his path.

"What are you doing!?" Saleem screamed, "Are you *crazy!?*"

Sharp turns threatened to send the sedan rolling into the forest, but Hassan held on tightly to his wheel. The speed breakers were the least of his worries and by the time he reached the entrance to the mountain slopes, there were no other cars daring to make such a dangerous climb.

Saleem looked into the back seat as Ali groaned. His skin, whatever still remained, had turned yellowed and discolored. With how faint he breathed, it appeared as if there was barely any time left for him. Saleem screamed at Hassan and shook his arm. He pleaded for him to return to Ali's home.

"His survival is important to me," Hassan said.

"You know they've destroyed the hospitals! His body is totally devastated," Saleem cried, "He won't survive. You're not even going the right way to the hospital!"

Hassan was calm, "I know where I'm going. This is the right direction."

Before Saleem had a moment to argue, a shockwave burst across the road nearly sending the sedan into the trees. As the two men looked into the sky, they saw it— the capsule-like drone. The sensors in the device were flashing erratically. The vehicle's speed caught their attention. And an ominous red light shone from the drone.

"We're going to die!" Saleem screamed, "It's over. It's over, over, over! We're dead! *DEAD!*"

"Shut up!" Hassan hollered, "I know what I'm doing. Today, you're going to see something you've never witnessed in your entire life."

Saleem gripped onto the dashboard for dear life, "When have I seen aliens before!? I've never even seen tanks or fighter planes exploding along the road! I've never seen *any* of this before in my life!"

As they spoke, the red beam on the drone grew in size and sent a blast towards the car. Hassan jutted the wheel and swerved away, nearly missing the attack. Hassan's chest pounded. He knew what needed to be done, but looking at the drone in front of him, he feared it wouldn't be possible.

"If this is what you've wanted to show me then I've seen in all already! Turn the car back! Now!" Saleem screamed again.

With another blast incoming, Hassan wove off of the road. The pedal had touched the floor. Mere centimeters stood between Hassan's car and the trees. He feared he would crash but he knew he had to go on. Not only did Ali's life depend on him, but if he couldn't escape the drone, they'd all be dead.

Blasts hit the trees, setting the forest ablaze. Even pushing his sedan to its maximum speed, the drone still lingered behind shooting its laser. It was inescapable. No matter how much he attempted to dodge, it was locked onto him.

"Oh shit. We're dead! We're dead, aren't we!? You've killed us, Hassan! Oh shit. Shit!"

Ignoring Saleem's wails, Hassan looked into the rearview mirror to see Ali, "Hang on! Stay with me!"

Further on the trail was a mud-filled track. Hassan went off-road, paying no mind to the sound of scraping branches. The further he drove, the darker the forest became. And even his headlights did little to improve his visibility. All he could do was push his car to its limits and travel onwards to the top of the mountain.

By the time Hassan noticed the river, it was already too late. His tires were spinning. Mud splashed into the air as the sedan began to sink. Panic emerged from both Hassan and Saleem. The drone was closing in and they were sitting defenseless.

"We have to run! Help me carry Ali!"

The two men poured out of the car and into the river. They bashed against the back door, trying to get it open to no avail. The window was the only option. They had mere moments until the drone gained on them, but they managed to pull Ali out of the car and carry him back onto land.

That, though, wasn't a moment they had to celebrate. The drone's laser landed a shot on the sedan, blasting metal bits into the air as it sank. Flames engulfed the vehicle. Saleem fell to the ground, overcome by fear. But Hassan pulled onto his shirt and motioned for him to continue onto the top of the mountain.

With Ali on his back and from the injuries he suffered during the wild ride, Hassan had difficulty running forward. But he soldiered on— he knew there was no other choice. They had made it past the river and only a short jog stood between them and the location that they sought.

"We've all gone mad. All people. All animals. Everyone and everything has gone *mad.* What are you trying to do? Bury him on top of a mountain? Do you *want* us to die to these aliens!?"

Hassan said nothing in response. He looked behind him and saw no sight of the drone. It had destroyed the car and that seemingly left it satisfied. From what he could tell, it was machines that attracted the aliens. And as they traveled up the rocky mountain pass, Hassan had to hope that they would remain safe.

Saleem's onslaught of frightened words was relentless. But Hassan paid him no mind. As they traveled further up the trail, the sun's light broke the darkness. At the top of the mountain stood a cave. The exterior was mossy and unassuming while the entrance showed less light than the forest from which they came.

As they took a final step to reach the peak, they heard an ear-wrenching explosion. Below them, they saw smoke and flames. If the damage to the sedan hadn't already been substantial enough, it was finally clear that the car would never drive again.

"Nice going!" Saleem mocked, "Now the car's destroyed. Guess we're just going to stay here until we *die.* We'll eat stones and drink from the river… hey! We can even live in that cave!"

Hassan grabbed his neck and hushed him. He pushed him forward toward the cave's entrance. Saleem gulped. They were going from one place of uncertainty to another. But at least in his eyes, this cave wasn't filled with drones looking to blast them into pieces.

While they traveled through the darkness, they noticed a glowing white light as they walked deeper. Both sides of the cave walls glowed with a faint light. And a chilling fog surrounded them. Despite the eeriness, there was peace within the cave. It was free of the chaotic sounds of the outside world. Only a faint hum resonated through the air.

"Amma Ji," Hassan called. *Dear old woman.*

The cave was silent. Hassan called out again. His eyes turned to the wall. The faint glow turned bright and the rocks shook. A passageway opened and from the hall came an old woman who walked with a long wooden stick.

Her hair was pure grey and her shrouded face was wrinkled but the old woman smiled as she saw Hassan. Though frail, the woman emanated confidence— she had no fear of her secluded home. And in her cloudy eyes, there was a sense of peace and wisdom.

Saleem, however, felt nothing but fright. He scurried backward, falling onto his rear. As he crawled away, he looked back at the old woman who locked her eyes on him. Those pupilless eyes— they scared Saleem. But as he studied her face, he saw no malice. She was a quaint old woman and reminded him of his own great-grandmother.

The old woman looked up at Hassan, "Why have you come back again?"

"My friend," Hassan said as he motioned towards Ali.

Sighing, the old woman said, "If your heart isn't pure, God will not help you."

Hassan pointed to Ali once again. His movements were more frantic, "My friend, Amma Ji. Help him."

Turning to face Ali, the woman lifted her walking stick in the air. She pointed towards the right wall which shook and glowed brighter. The white light turned a vibrant shade of green. Such mysticism was a mystery to Saleem who cowered in the corner. But for Hassan, it brought him back to that day eight years ago.

He recalled her words back then, "If your heart is not pure, God will not help you. But whatever does happen will be the will of God."

"I am ready," he replied.

The old woman laughed, "Many warriors came here believing they were prepared but were burned to ash, my son."

Returning inside the cave, she said, "Are you sure?"

At the time, Hassan didn't truly know what he was getting himself into. He saw the skeletons at his feet. He knew what she meant by 'burned to ash'. But he was strong in his faith. He believed nothing was going to stand in his way from his goal.

He saw the green light glowing through the cave. And he knew its source— the crystal. The old woman's voice still echoed in his mind, "Are you sure? Are you sure?" Though, back then, his resolve wavered. The sound of her voice overwhelming his mind— he couldn't handle it.

Hassan ran. By the time his feet touched the mouth of the cave, he felt a blast behind him. He screamed as the green light surrounded him. He was swept along by the light as if it were a rope. It wrapped itself around his arms and legs, carrying him through the forest.

He was sent cascading through the trees until he reached the river. There, he fell into the river where his body beat into the passing rocks before washing ashore. Hassan believed he would have died there. And truly, he would have. But Ali was there. Ali spotted him along the river and carried him to the hospital.

Though his consciousness was limited, Hassan knew what he saw. The green light that was inside his own body transferred to Ali. The light went to those who were pure. And from that moment forward, Hassan knew that it was Ali whose heart was purer than any other.

But the roles were reversed. It was now Hassan's turn to save Ali and he vowed he would do whatever it took. He laid his friend down beside the green crystal. The magic that it held was a mystery even to him. But he had faith that it could help Ali.

Saleem still held skepticism. As he took a step forward, he heard a crunch beneath his feet and stumbled backward. His eyes widened— he saw a human skull. Screaming at the top of his lungs, he rushed to Hassan and pulled him out of the cave. In his mind, the green light and the crystal was going to be their doom.

In Hassan's mind, he heard the voice playing in his head, "Are you sure?"

Looking back, he spotted the old woman. She returned inside the cave wall from which she came. She was silent, but her voice echoed in Hassan's mind. It was calming. For once, Hassan felt no fear. If he could trust anyone to be pure of heart, he knew he could trust Ali.

He smiled, "I am sure."

SCENE XXII

His body was charred. He no longer had any sensation in his limbs. His vision and hearing— they were both gone. But Ali's mind was still working. While he couldn't comprehend the outside world, his thoughts kept going back to his days in the army. It was so long ago and yet… the devastation felt so familiar.

The war between Pakistan and India was a brutal one. Missiles landed into civilian villages, slaughtering all who inhabited them. No one was spared. The soldiers watched as their friends and loved ones were slaughtered alongside them. And they could only think of revenge.

Ali remembered the bunker. He and his squad pushed up towards the outer wall. When gunfire was exchanged, neither side was spared. Soldier's from Ali's own squad dropped beside him. And on India's side, there were few who remained standing. It was a complete bloodbath.

Fires raged on, burning the corpses that lay out in front of the bunker. And amongst the smoke and screaming, Ali heard a faint voice sobbing. At first, he believed the voice belonged to a child. But as he moved closer, he noticed that it was a young Indian soldier.

The young man crawled out from the pile of corpses. Tears and blood stained his cheeks. He lifted both of his hands and held them into the air. Ali's eyes locked onto the soldier. He couldn't have been much older than eighteen. And from the way he shook, this was his first time experiencing death.

"Please. I swear to God I've never fired a shot. I just joined the army… it's barely been a month. If you let me go… I'll- I'll run away. I'll leave the army. Please! Look at my hands. I have no weapon!"

"Shut up!" the commanding officer screamed as he kicked the boy to the ground, "Ali. Kill him."

Ali froze. Seeing the young man in front of him—the young boy —he couldn't accept any more death. Standing before a fellow human and watching him sob and beg, Ali refused to continue the cycle of hurt. But he knew, too, that his commanding officer didn't allow for dissension.

The officer threw Ali a knife, "Be a soldier. Kill him."

But Ali let the knife drop onto the ground. He refused to pick it up and take part in any more destruction. Between the young man's strained cries and the commanding officer's shouting, Ali couldn't think. He struggled to breathe. He wanted the nightmare to be over.

"Kill him!" the voice rang in Ali's head, "Kill him!"

And among the chaos, the young soldier lunged forward and reached for the knife. Ali was motionless. He watched as the boy pulled him down and sliced the blade into his chest. At that moment, despite the pain he felt, Ali couldn't move. In the young man's eyes, he saw fear instead of malice.

But the soldier paused. Blood dripped from his lips. The officer fired bullets into the boy, riddling his body full of holes. Ali watched as the scared soldier was reduced to a mangled corpse. And as the boy's body collapsed, Ali knew then and there that he could no longer bear to be in the army.

When his commanding officer asked Ali if he was alright, he was at a loss for words. Covered in blood—not only just his own blood —Ali was sickened. He had known the horrors that came with war. But this was far too much.

He rose to his feet. As the commanding officer extended his hand, Ali slapped it away, "No more killing! No more war!"

His throat was raw as he screamed. He had enlisted to protect his country, but he learned that he was only participating in more hurt. Ali wanted his fellow soldiers to understand. He wanted to show everyone that their methods of war were only further denying any chance of peace. But instead, Ali was court-martialed.

A dim sound pulled Ali out of his dream. It was a voice. But it was one he didn't recognize. A woman was speaking to him. She had a frail and raspy voice that was calming and motherly. Light gave way to darkness. Ali was able to see once more, but what he saw terrified him.

Beneath him was his body— it was charred beyond repair. His limbs were torn apart from his body. He had no eyes nor fingers and his blood flowed along the rock piles of the cave. Ali didn't understand how he was seeing everything in front of him. He questioned if he was dead. And as he noticed the green light emanating around him, he believed he had become a spirit.

Hassan and Saleem ran from the cave as the green light chased them. He listened as the voice asked Hassan, "Are you sure?" incessantly. But he understood none of it. All he knew was that he was alone peering down at his own body. He believed everything was already over.

"You don't want to fight, but the fight has now come to you," said a deep voice, different from that of the old woman, "You don't want to kill, but now you are the one dying."

Ali searched for the source of the man's voice but found nothing. Though, the voice was cheerful even in such trying times. Ali wanted to believe that the voice was there to help him. The sound continued, "This is not your fight. This is not the fight of your country. This is the fight of all of humanity. And if you want, you can save it. But whatever happens, will be the will of God."

"If it is the will of God," Ali was hesitant, "What difference does it make if I say 'yes' or 'no'? If I try or if I don't try, won't fate happen as intended anyway?"

The voice replied, "That's why God has given humanity a choice. Whatever you choose, you will be paving your own path. This is not an order. You can choose to ignore it. If not you, then there will be another. The responsibility is huge. It is the heaviest burden you will ever face, my son. But it is a choice you are given."

As Ali tried to make sense of what the voice was saying, he felt pain. It wasn't his own body that ached. He sensed the pain taking place outside the cave. Humans were dying. All of humanity bled and wept. And his own body was taking its final breaths.

"You only have a few more minutes."

Ali looked down at his body. His breathing was strained. Death was inevitable. But he wondered about the choice the voice gave him. If he agreed, would he live? Would he be given a second chance to protect his family? That thought alone meant more to him than anything.

But from the way the voice talked, it was more than just his own family who needed to be protected. All of humanity was endangered. There were animals, fields of vibrant flowers, forests of trees— the beauty of all life was threatened by an unknown enemy.

He calmed his mind. He knew whatever he was getting himself into would be far beyond anything he ever knew. But the voice's words haunted him. If he chose not to do it, would someone else be forced to carry the same burden? Ali didn't wish for such weight to fall on anyone.

Ali's answer was clear, "I'll do it."

Just as he spoke those words, the crystal's green light became blinding. It wove into the air and cast kaleidoscopic images onto the cave wall. As the light entered Ali's body, he felt warmth. He felt life once more. And beyond the ability to breathe, he felt energy surging from every part of himself.

Beside him, more of the green light collected to form the shape of a human body. Though, the figure was smaller in size. The form was that of an old man with a long white beard. On his head sat a tall cylindrical white hat. And his clothing— a long tunic and robe —was stark white and earthy green.

The old man whirled as Ali watched the spirit split in two. What began as two whirling figures multiplied into four and then sixteen. Soon, there were hundreds of green spirits dancing around his body. Ali knew the spirits reminded him of something. It was a word Hassan often spoke of— Darwaish.

SCENE XXIII

Saleem wailed as he hid his face and sat outside the cave, "I don't understand this. I don't understand anything. You brought me into a no-man's zone. And you're making me crazy! You're going to kill me!"

Hassan sighed, "Shh! If the drones hear us we'll *really* be dead."

But that did little to comfort Saleem, "We came all the way to bring Ali to this place and now we're just waiting outside. Who was that old woman? Did you see her eyes!? I've taken some stuff before, but nothing has ever made me high like this."

Seeing Hassan remain still and quiet, Saleem continued to speak, "If the aliens don't kill us, we're still going to die from the cold or hunger or-"

He yelped as a sharp, fast object flew past his ear and shattered into the rocks. Looking behind him, he saw a stray bullet falling to the ground. Pieces of the rock broke from the wall sending pebbles pelting his cheek. As he touched his face, he felt blood. Saleem screamed.

From the burning forest, the capsule-like drone emerged. Hassan's breathing seized. He had thought they were safe secluded by the cave. He grabbed Saleem and pulled him down to the ground, hoping that the drone hadn't locked on to the two of them.

It baffled him how the drone was able to find them. From what he knew, the aliens were attracted to machines and weapons. He didn't know what could have called them to their location. And then it hit him. The stray bullet wasn't from the drone at all. They were sitting across from the Indian border.

"Ahh! What the-" Saleem cried before Hassan covered his mouth.

Hassan was quiet but stern, "We're in the middle of the line of control. You're moving around and making a scene. The snipers saw you."

Sweat poured down Saleem's face, "Yeah… that's all I needed. That's all that was left. Why did you bring me here!? It's death everywhere! Up and down. From my front to my back..."

Saleem dug his fingers into his skin. His voice turned frantic, "I need my drugs. I'm going to die. I'm actually going to die. And it's your fault. I'll kill you!"

As Hassan called to Saleem to calm down, the young worker picked up a flat rock with a sharp edge. From raising his voice, the drone had turned to face him. The red light shone brightly. In a panic, Hassan grabbed him and dragged him towards the cave.

With the drone on their trail, Hassan feared all hope was lost. They couldn't outrun it and if they led it into the cave, they'd only endanger Ali further. Hassan stopped. Whatever fate had in store for him, he knew he had to accept it. He locked eyes with the drone.

But before the red light had a chance to form itself into a beam, it flipped into the air and swung like a pendulum. Gaining speed, the drone crashed into the mountainside and shattered into metallic shards. It happened so fast that Hassan didn't have time to comprehend what was happening.

Their eyes widened with shock. A flow of green light wafted through the air. It swirled and danced before manifesting into a human form. Neither of them could believe their eyes. A human was standing before them. And that human had emerged from a ray of light.

It was Ali.

His body— once charred —was dripping blood was strong and healthy. There was not a single mark on his body. Even the scars he had from years ago— the knife wounds on his chest —were completely gone. He was tall and muscular far more than he had ever been.

Ali stepped towards them and Saleem panicked. Before the young worker had a chance to speak, Ali reached out and pressed his hand on the man's heart. Green glowing light flowed through Saleem's veins and all the fear and pain he felt slowly faded away. He was calm.

As Saleem looked up at Ali, a single tear fell from his eye. It was not one of sorrow. For once during the chaotic day, the young worker felt joy. Something was assuring him that all would be well. And while he couldn't fully understand it, he could feel it in his heart.

Saleem looked at Hassan, "You… you were right. What I've seen and felt today is unlike anything I've experienced before."

But while the three were reunited, all was not yet at peace. Another bullet flew through the air and gust past Ali. Before the two men had a chance to react, they saw Ali's arm extend. Between his fingers, he held a single bullet. There was no struggle or sight of pain. And Ali didn't even face the direction from which the bullet came.

"Oh… oh my God!" Saleem gasped, "You're like a superhero. It's like from the movies. Am I dreaming? Oh no… I'm dreaming! "

Ali paid no mind to Saleem who continued to rant and rave. In the sky, he watched a group of capsule-like drones fly towards the location of the sniper. He knew that beyond the bushes and trees, the Indian army was waiting. They were frightened and desperate. And he knew they'd been ill-prepared for the on-coming attack. He had to do something.

Scene XXIV

In a small room inside the depths of the cave, the old woman sat. She twirled her walking stick in her hands as she stared up at a faint white light. Her expression was calm but she furrowed her brows. Waving her stick in hand, she spoke to the light that began to grow.

"He's not ready yet," she said.

The man's voice responded, "He didn't come to us himself. We had no time to prepare him. It is unlike we did with the previous ones. We tried our best with the ones before him. Nothing remains forever but God."

The old woman was not convinced. Her mind was filled with thoughts of the past. And as she thought, all of the light and calmness turned to darkness and chaos. There was much she wished to caution Ali about his new burden. But as the voice said, they didn't have any time.

She thought of an old man with a white beard. At that time, he was just as weak and frail. He wished to be filled with the power of the green light. His greed for power was insurmountable. And when he was denied for having a heart filled with impurities, he didn't take the refusal kindly.

It was the next turn of events that left her worried. The old man's face contorted into anger. His face, once serene and wrinkled, had been overtaken by shadows. Darkness surrounded him. He became the absence of light. As he looked upon the Green Darwaishs that whirled, he slaughtered them.

"This time, let him learn everything himself," the man said, "Maybe it is best for him right now.. He will come to understand the world."

And even from where she sat, the old woman could see him. She watched Ali as he sat atop the mountain. His eyes were closed and he was at peace. When he focused, he could absorb the world around him. He felt everything that happened within the Earth.

As the planet spun, Ali felt himself sway. As the sun's rays shone down, he understood their warmth. Whether it was the moon's light or ocean's waves, Ali felt connected. He sensed every bird that spread their wings. And he felt the breathing of every fish that jumped from the water.

There was beauty in the world. That was something Ali always knew in his heart. But at that moment, he truly understood. He reached out his palm to collect fallen snow and windswept bits of pine. As he held it in his hands, it was as near to him as the heartbeat of every human.

The spirit said to the old woman, "Let him settle this with himself. Rest. God knows best."

Scene XXV

With his eyes closed, Ali was able to focus and take in the world around him. It was mesmerising to have all of the world's beautiful coursing through his veins. He felt everyone's laughter and joy. But at the same time, he sensed everyone's pain. That in itself devastated Ali.

Behind him, Saleem snuck up with the flat rock in hand. He couldn't believe his eyes. Nothing about any of the day made sense to him. But especially, he couldn't believe that his own boss had turned into what he could only assume was a superhero. There was something Saleem needed to confirm.

Saleem lunged at Ali with the sharpened rock, expecting him to dodge out of the way at lightning speed. He wanted to see what he witnessed before with the drone and the bullet. He wanted to confirm that Ali did indeed have strength and speed beyond any man.

But as Saleem thrust forward, the rock halted. It smashed into Ali's stomach sending particles of stone cascading through the air. Saleem gasped. Ali opened his eyes. He tilted his head as he watched Saleem who skipped backward and tripped over his own feet.

"S-s- sorry! I'm sorry! I wanted to check if I was dreaming," Saleem scrambled to his feet, "But you were blown up so… I figured a rock or a knife or something wouldn't be… you know."

Ali smiled and looked to Hassan who cackled. He was happy to see his friends in good spirits. He knew the pain and turmoil they went through to bring him atop the mountain. For that, he was grateful. Being able to make them smile was the very least he could do. But still, he wished to do more.

Checking the sky, the drones had surrounded the Indian army. Their side of the line of control was overwhelmed by drones. And a battle had begun. Lasers, missiles, guns, and flames— war was continuing on. Ali pointed to the chaos, alerting his friends.

"Good!" Saleem screamed, "I hope they all die! India has been killing our soldiers for far too long. It's time that-"

Ali held up his hand to halt him, "No. These are not just Indians. These are *humans*."

Before either Saleem or Hassan had a chance to say another word, Ali had taken a step towards the cliff's edge. His feet hovered. As his friends watched in shock,

Ali rose into the air and flew towards the onslaught. Alongside him, a tiny army of thousands of bearded men surrounded him— the Green Darwaish.

Ali watched as his small army danced and whirled around him. He smiled. Whatever power it was that the crystal and the glowing light gave him, Ali knew he needed to put it to the test. This was now the responsibility and burden he bore. And with one last kick of his legs, Ali took off with a sonic blast towards the drones.

SCENE XXVI

Panic broke out from the line of soldiers as lasers and missiles overwhelmed them. And despite their attempts to fight back, the drones locked onto their guns and shot down all and anyone who attempted to fight back. It was no battle— it was a bloodbath.

On one side, the Indian army struggled to keep their footing while the drones threatened to wipe them out. And that wasn't their only enemy. Soldiers from Pakistan, in a panic, rushed through the mountains. The sniper from India's side put them on full alert. And as they attempted to defend themselves, the drones left them scattered.

The aliens didn't discriminate, they shot all and any who held a weapon. And by the time both sides of the battle understood that, it was already too late. They became more frantic in their assault, emptying entire magazines in hopes of driving off the drones. But in the end, it only caused more of the capsule-like machines to flock to them.

In the chaos, the line of control had been crossed. The border was no longer of concern to either side when lasers and missiles threatened to gun them down. It may have been the Indian sniper that first alerted the Pakistani side, but now that the aliens had surrounded them, they had no choice but to leave their stations.

As the battle continued on, scientists from the UN office watched as the line of defense was overwhelmed by drones. They wished to send aid. But even if they were able to mobilize a unit to protect the troops, there was nothing they had that could hold back the aliens.

"What is happening?" the general said, "They're drawing more drones to themselves. What are they doing!?"

He closed his eyes as a lone Pakistani soldier fired his gun only to be shot down by a laser. His flesh melted and his blood boiled. In minutes, he was reduced to nothing more than a pile of gore. And the same could be said for the forest itself. Trees caught fire— pine needles became floating embers.

The environment itself became a death trap. Soldiers ducked and dodged as tree trunks shattered around them. Charred branches fell to the ground. And watching the devastation around him, a lone soldier wailed as he found himself cornered. Between flames, enemy soldiers, drones, and falling timber, he had nowhere to turn.

Tears streamed down his cheeks as he watched a drone fly towards him. He believed it was the end. He believed he was going to die. In his panic, the man didn't even notice the large fallen branch beside him float into the air.

The drone went flying. The man gasped. He didn't know what was happening. And as he looked beside himself, he was only more confused. A tall, muscular man holding the remains of a charred tree batted the drone away like a baseball. And if witnessing the act once was unbelievable in itself, the soldier watched Ali perform the feat over and over.

Flying into the air like a baseball superstar, Ali whacked the drone into each other, causing them to burst. It was the explosion of bits of metal gears and parts that alerted the soldiers to the spectacle above them. Their eyes went wide as they pointed into the sky. In their entire lives, they have never seen anything like it.

While the soldiers saw Ali alone, only he knew that he was accompanied by the Green Darwaish. The moment he picked up the branch, each of the whirling spirits manifested one as well. And when he swung his makeshift bat, each of them joined him in smashing the drones into bits.

"Who… who are you!?" a soldier screamed.

"…I don't know yet," Ali said as he held his finger to his mouth, "Shh."

The answer to that question was one even he didn't know himself. Continuing on his onslaught, bashing the capsule-like drones through the sky, Ali had to wonder what he truly *was* any longer. The power he possessed was more than any man. But he still retained his own thoughts and mind.

Fighting back, the drones shot lasers at the branches, setting them ablaze. Though, just as easily as the Darwaish spawned the manifestations, they were able to create new ones. At last, the drones were the ones left defenseless. As long as he controlled the Green Darwaish, Ali believed he could stop anything.

Back at Geneva's UN office, everyone was in an uproar. Their satellites had gone down, preventing them from having a proper image. But for the first time, they knew that the drones were being pushed back. Their data showed that the Pakistani and Indian armies had run together and ended up holed up around the same location.

By all accounts, the UN officials believed the soldiers would wipe each other out while the aliens finished off the rest. But from what their readings were showing, it was the drones who were getting pushed back. And as each of the scientists sat anxiously around the boardroom screen, they wished to finally see what was happening at the border of Kashmir.

"We're getting the satellites back up now," Anna said as she pointed to the screen, "Wait for it in five... four... three... two... one..."

When the images were in front of them, the entire room was shocked. But despite that images being far beyond what they ever imagined to be possible, they were awe-inspiring. Finally, humanity had a hero—someone who could stand up against the aliens when no one else could.

It appeared to be magic. That was the only way everyone in the room could describe what they were seeing. A muscular man was flying through the air with a giant tree branch batting away the drones. And if that didn't surprise them enough, there was what seemed to be a hundred more logs swinging in the air by themselves.

Only Ali knew the true nature of what was occurring. Though, even he couldn't fully explain what it was that he was doing. It was a sense and a feeling. Just like he was able to sense all of the natural world around him, he was able to use his powers to protect all of humanity.

As he fought, though, Ali felt goosebumps on the back of his neck. His ears were ringing. He had incredible power, but it was not unlimited. He watched as more drones flew down from the sky above. Just as he was able to replenish his Green Darwaishs, the aliens were replenishing their numbers as well.

The ringing in his ears persisted. Something was coming. Hearing the sound of snarls and howls, it finally dawned on Ali what else was still lurking through the forest. And as he looked through the burning trees, he spotted what appeared to be a thousand rabid dogs barreling through the mountains.

Along with barking, he heard human screams. The soldiers were running scared and they were cornered. In front of them was a sky full of drones. And behind them was a pack of vicious dogs. With their defenses weakened, they believed they finally met their end. But Ali refused to let that happen.

Soaring away with another sonic blast, Ali crashed between the soldiers and the dogs. Pushing his palms forward, he moved a quick whipping gust of air that knocked rows of dogs off of their feet. While his new power truly felt all-encompassing, Ali was finally starting to see his limits.

As he struggled with the dogs, the Darwaish fought the drones. But without his energy pulsing through them, they were unable to regenerate. The aliens were pushing back. The more they fired, the more of the Darwaish numbers were dwindling. Ali needed to think fast. Everything was coming undone.

Drones broke past the whirling army and set their sights on the soldiers. Fleeing for their lives, the soldiers had limited space to run. They shoved and climbed their way through the mountain passes but found no escape from their enemies that wished to destroy them. And just before they believed that nothing could make matters worse…

Crrrrraaccckkk

An Indian soldier gasped as he felt the ground beneath his feet opening. It was a landslide, or at least, that was the only explanation the armies had for the rocks and soil breaking apart. The skies above were a danger but now the Earth itself wished to take them.

Falling into the crack, the Indian soldier wailed. He thrashed and grabbed stones and roots, desperately trying to save himself. But he was slipping. Tired and sore, he hadn't the strength left to hold himself above ground. And he feared he'd succumb to whatever depths lurked below.

Before he could slip any further, the Indian soldier saw a hand reach down to him. Instinctively, he grabbed it. He believed one of his fellow troops had come to his rescue. But he felt shocked as he spotted the insignia— two swords below a star and crescent. It was a Pakistani soldier rescuing him.

At that moment, all of the resentment he held for his enemy had turned to thankfulness. They were no longer enemies but two humans fighting for survival. Humanity relied on brotherhood. In times of chaos and struggle, having many hands coming together was what the world needed most. Peace was the most they could strive to uphold.

And sensing that pure heart and spirit inspired Ali. He closed his eyes and sensed the world around him. Instead of fighting the dogs, he tried to understand them. He breathed in deeply, feeling their fear. He sent a flow of green light through each of them.

When he opened his eyes, the dogs' bloodshot eyes had cleared. They no longer barred their teeth or hunched their backs. The dogs were calm— confused, yet in a place of peace. They dispersed through the forest, running past the flames and drones and leaving the soldiers alone.

Peering up at the skies again, Ali knew he still had the drones to contend with. He picked up another burning tree stump and blasted into the air. He had united warring factions, pacified vicious beasts, and now he knew his final step would be driving back the aliens. But he knew that last step wouldn't be easy. There were still aliens all over the world.

Not only were there millions of capsule-like drones in every city in the world, but just outside the Earth's atmosphere, there was a ship floating through space. Much like the drones themselves, the mothership was sleek and cylindrical in shape. But inside weren't just mindless machines, the brains of the operation sat at a command station watching battles on Earth take place.

He was a fearsome creature— a large bulbous face with white veiny skin and beady slits for eyes. He clenched his jaw, shattering bits of green-tinted teeth and sending them flying across the station. He saw everything that took place at the line of defense. And he refused to let anything stand in the way of his plans.

Taking a long metallic staff with a glowing pink crystal in hand, the alien commander wailed aloud, frightening the smaller beings who worked around him.

Each of the tiny aliens ran between the control panels and the sliding doors. They geared and suited themselves for battle.

The docking bay of the ship opened and more drones burst down to Earth at rapid speeds. But it wasn't only the tiny aliens who led the assault. The commander shouted to his workers to lower the ship. It was time for them to finally break into Earth's atmosphere.

Hovering his massive clawed hands over a red button, the alien commander smiled. A small alien called out to him. *The cannons are ready.* And from the moment he pressed the button, it was as if the Earth's rotation had halted. Everything was moving in slow motion as the beam came down.

In the skies above Shanghai, the very last sight anyone saw was a warm red ray of light. Heat overwhelmed the city, melting towers and building into pools of molten metal. All life was annihilated before it had a chance to react. In seconds, one of the world's major cities was gone.

And while all of that happened, Ali felt sharp pains all over his body. Without knowing anything about the tragedy that occurred, he was able to sense the devastation. Somewhere in the world, millions of people were wiped away in an instant. Their beating hearts were only a faint memory.

Ali gasped, "Oh my God… I… I can't do this alone. I need help."

His powers were still a mystery even to him, but Ali believed that there was something he could do. He located gathering of humans— the ones that were watching from a satellite. He could sense them. Their hearts were beating from their chests. He needed to go to them.

Closing his eyes once more, Ali imagined the location. It was a small room with a video screen. There were people from all walks of life and many different countries. They had to be planning something, he thought. And if he could work together with them, Ali was certain he could save humanity.

As he opened his eyes, the thought of the room flashed through his mind once more. And with just one more breath, Ali vanished.

The old woman furrowed her brow once more. These were trying times. Ali had only just begun to understand the power he possessed. And he was forced to use it to hold back a threat that meant to destroy all of humanity. She hoped that he was prepared.

Teleportation was not an ability Ali knew that he had. But just like with his other powers, it came naturally to him as he focused his mind and his energy. But while he was learning how to control himself, he was unsure how to explain his gifts to anyone else.

Standing in front of the table of scientists, he understood their fears. They screamed and called for the guards who promptly opened fire on him. The bullets were of no consequence to Ali, but he knew he was going to have to help everyone to understand why he had appeared before them.

"Calm down," he said, "I'm here to help."

Those words got the guards to lower their weapons, but there was still skepticism. Ali wanted to break the ice. He pointed to the screen, "You've been watching me all this time. I know you're at least somewhat impressed. Let me explain everything. At least, let me explain that I'm here to help you."

Pacified, the lead scientist, Anna, asked Ali to go on, "You've seen me fight the aliens. But you know as well as I do that there are too many. I need your help too. We need to form an army. We need to gather whatever weapons humanity has left to make a final stand."

Ali's eyes darted to a sign that read 'Development and Peace', "All of you have been working towards peace. We can work towards it together. The drones target weapons. When they sense a machine or weapon, they lock on. But I have a plan."

"We don't have much time," Ali said before Anna could interject, "We need to move quickly. I will keep the drones engaged. Meanwhile, I need you all to mobilize every army and defense system you have. We need to get all civilians out of the city. No major city is safe. You will bring your weapons and I will bring the rain. We must fight together. Together as one— humanity must stand up."

But despite his worlds, there were still doubts. The scientists wished to know who or *what* he was. They feared he was one of the aliens as well. And general grumbled that a stranger would barge into the UN and demand that they mobilize their weapons. It seemed as if no one was on his side.

Though, there was one who wished to give him the benefit of the doubt. Anna, she rose to her feet and stood before Ali. She saw what he was capable of. She watched all that he had accomplished through the screen and she wanted to believe that he was the hero the world needed.

Ali placed his hand on the woman's heart. Just as he had done with Saleem, he let green light pulse through her veins. All of the sorrow and hurt she felt dissipated. She felt calm and hopeful. Most importantly, she truly believed that Ali would be the one to stop the alien invasion.

"Who are you?" she asked.

"I am the protector of all."

Without saying another word, Ali teleported back to the line of control. He couldn't leave the soldiers stranded. And he was certain that the UN knew what to do. Anna had felt his light and he trusted that she would carry on his message.

The UN members were unsure, but they knew that Ali had been the only one to even stand a fighting chance against the drones. If he had a plan, that was more than anything else they could hope. They had assumed the world was doomed, but humanity finally had a shot to prosper.

Calling other headquarters, the UN rallied armies and advanced weapons together. But they weren't the only ones preparing for another assault. The mothership had risen back into space, but their cannons were preparing to strike the next major city. Even they knew they needed to move quickly. They saw Ali's plan in action.

Sensing the changes in the air, that's when it finally hit Ali. He felt the ship leaving the atmosphere and he blasted off into the sky to track it down. He didn't know what he was getting himself into when he chased it, but if destroying the ship would prevent more deaths, he needed to try.

As Ali flew through the atmosphere and into space, however, he felt his body weakening. The strength of his body faltered. He could no longer sense and feel the world around him— everything went dark. And as Ali pushed forward, he began to fall. His mind was racing. *"Did I lose my power?"*

Falling faster, Ali was in a panic. But the closer he came to the ground, he felt the green energy surging back inside of him. His strength returned. He could sense and feel everything again. Just before he crashed into the Earth, it finally dawned on him— his powers were connected to the planet itself.

On Earth, he had more power than he could ever imagine. But the enemy he faced was in space. "What do

I do? How do I destroy the mothership?" While he was first filled with confidence, Ali began to doubt if what he sought was even possible. He had to hope that the UN would be able to pull through too.

Landing back at the line of control, Ali noticed that the number of drones had doubled. Just when he thought he had driven them back, they returned with even greater numbers. He watched as a drone flashed its red light and locked onto the row of soldiers. They were all in danger.

Ali leapt in front of the missile, sending his body rolling and crashing into the trees. As he stood, his body was burnt from head to toe. But the damage did not last. Walking back to the capsule-like drone, Ali's body healed until he had no marks or scars. The aliens may not have been able to damage him, but he couldn't say the same for the soldiers.

"There's too many," he thought, "If I keep fighting here, the soldiers will be killed."

Eyeing the blast-proof door of a destroyed bunker, Ali lifted it. Just as they had done with the tree branches, the Green Darwaishs manifested similar doors. As Ali flew, the whirling old men joined him. He made a shield in the sky before shouting to the soldiers.

"Run away! Get out of here! Drop all of your weapons and run. The aliens can detect your guns!"

Talking amongst each other, the soldiers couldn't believe what was happening. But they wanted to trust Ali. From everything they had witnessed, he was a hero.

If anyone was going to save them, they believed it was going to be Ali.

"Do what he says! Listen to Qalandar!"

"Qalandar will save us!"

"Put your faith in Qalandar!"

Drones continued to blast and break away the shields, but Ali held the defense. He and the Darwaish protected the skies as the soldiers fled down the mountain. But as he held the line, Ali began to feel tired. He was using the limits of his strength and stretching his power as far as it could go.

Seeing the last of the soldiers either reach the mountain base or cram into the tunnels, Ali took a moment to breathe. As he loosened his grip on the makeshift shield, the Darwaish began to vanish. He was falling. No longer could he keep his body afloat and he felt his limbs crash into the bushes and branches around him. He was without any energy, but he was calm.

Hidden among the bushes, he had a reprieve from the drones' attacks. They zipped through the forest in search of weapons but found them idle. Ali had a moment to regain his composure and health. Nestled amongst nature, he was able to close his eyes and take in the energy of the world.

But time was not a luxury Ali had. The mothership was breaking through Earth's atmosphere yet again. It was dropping towards the line of defense and its cannons were fueling up to launch another devastating blow. Ali took a deep breath and stood. His rest was short, but it was enough to refill him with the power he needed.

The next bomb was going to be in Kashmir. Ali refused to let that happen. He knew the ship was targeting him. He needed to avert their attention. Ali picked up a fallen rifle and shot it in the air. That was the calling card he needed to have every drone on the mountain on his trail.

Ali flew into the air, shooting the rifle at the drones to keep them taunted. He had to find an abandoned area. His mind searched for a strip of barren land. That would be the battlefield while the armies in Geneva prepared their weapons. Ali just had to hope that the plan would work.

Scene XXVII

Back at the UN office, there was an uproar. Teams had called to every country in the world to send their aid. Humanity was finally taking back their home. But the preparations were leaving the offices stressed. Just gearing up and mobilizing alone left them in danger. They had to hope that Ali could protect them long enough to rally their troops.

The border to France was barricaded by rows of tanks and soldiers. Any civilian left in Geneva had been escorted into the French countryside by the military. All other bases were asked to stand down to keep the fight isolated in Switzerland. This was humanity's last line of defense.

There were units stationed along the trails leading up to the alps focused on clearing the skies from rogue drones sneaking past the mountains. The harbor's ships were under military control, but even fit with torpedos, they were no match for the onslaught of missiles that sought to sink them.

Along with the UN office, the botanical gardens and Temple de Saint-Pierre were the last locations safe from the rain of lasers and bullets. Soldiers had their backs against the wall. The morale was low. Any moment running through the city streets meant that one may be giving their lives to keep the world safe. And while many wished to protect their friends and loved ones, few were prepared to pay the ultimate price.

Anna pointed to an incoming threat on their radar. The mothership— the monstrosity that left all of Shanghai in ruins had breached the atmosphere once more. And this time, it appeared to be dropping along the border of Kashmir where Ali fought waves of drones.

He had certainly done what he had promised. Teams from around the world reported that the number of drones had decreased. They were all going to Ali. Every drone was on its way to intersect and finish him off. He was giving humanity an opportunity to regroup, but the scientists worried how long he could hold out.

"What's our status on the missiles? We need them ready before those cannons strike again!"

Four massive launchers were what the UN team hoped would be enough to stop the mothership. It was all they had left since the drones wiped out so much of their defenses. But they didn't doubt the destructive force of the missiles. It would blast and turn anything they could imagine into bits. And if it didn't, they had to hope that Ali would be there to wrap up the rest.

Even with Ali acting as bait, there were still drones drawn to the military's movement. The numbers were split and dwindling, but the armies were far from safe. Reaching Geneva was going to be a feat in itself and time was not on anyone's side. They couldn't predict when the alien cannons would be ready to launch again.

And their situation was becoming grimmer as even the alien commander noticed Ali's plan. He couldn't determine what Ali was, but he was certainly a stronger force than any human he had witnessed. The alien commander screamed to his workers to target the UN base in Geneva, he saw the military movement and knew something was about to go down.

But he knew he could not ignore Ali. With only a single rifle, Ali was able to summon his Green Darwaish and launch an assault as if he had thousands of soldiers behind him. The drones sparked and fell from the sky as their fuses were destroyed. Between Geneva and Ali, the commander didn't know which to destroy first.

Veins burst from the alien's pale head as he rose to his feet with a deafening roar. His eyes had turned red and seeped blood. But even in his fit of rage, he knew what to do. He smashed his knuckles together as he stared at Ali on his monitor. It was finally time to wipe out his enemy.

SCENE XXVIII

Shooting into the crowd of drones, Ali's eyes suddenly went wide. The rifle was out of bullets, but he couldn't give up. He snapped off pieces from the gun and tossed it at the drones. The Green Darwaishs followed suit. Using anything and everything at his disposal, Ali continued to attack.

"There's so many," he thought to himself, *"I don't know if Geneva can handle them all."*

The desert landscape was in total chaos. Lasers and bullets kicked up the sands creating a crater in the barren Earth. Ali knew he had to hang on. He needed to buy time for the UN to rally the world's armies. But as he fought the drones, he felt a faint wind blowing.

Goosebumps ran down his neck. He could sense that something was amiss, but his mind couldn't pinpoint it. He wanted to close his eyes and peer through the world, but he couldn't distract himself from the fight. His heart pounded. Something was coming, but he didn't understand what it could be.

Pain radiated across Ali's face. Before he knew what hit him, he was sent flying across the desert. Only the burning sands were there to slow his fall as he tumbled for what seemed like kilometers. Despite his torn and bleeding skin, Ali was able to heal. But as he looked up, he was met with a menacing sight.

Wiping the blood from his mouth, Ali locked eyes with the alien commander. The being wore a gold-plated suit that seemed to give the alien the ability of flight. Ali was at a loss for words. He had never seen anything like the plaster-white beast with bulging veins. And before he had a chance to figure out a strategy, the alien was lunging back at him for a second assault.

Just from one punch alone, Ali was weakened. And as he looked around, the drones were dispersing. He knew that the UN was no longer safe and he needed to act fast. His plan of being a diversion was failing. As long as the massive beast was there before him, he wouldn't be able to keep the drones occupied.

But since it was flesh in front of him instead of a machine, Ali had an idea. Just as he had done with Saleem, he wondered if he could look into the alien's heart. Just as he had done with the rabid dogs, he wondered if he could ease the hatred and fear the being possessed.

Teleporting behind the alien, Ali placed his hand on the being's chest. He hoped to find a heart. He knew if he could look into the alien's thoughts and emotions, he could find a solution that would bring peace. Ali closed his eyes and he searched, surging green light through the commander's body.

As Ali searched, though, he was shocked. Instead of any shred of life or love, he felt nothing but darkness. Inside the alien commander was only hatred. There was no hope for light. There was no hope for peace. The only thing the alien desired was destruction.

Listening to the alien's thoughts, Ali learned his final plan. The alien's wanted to wipe all life from Earth. To them, humanity was a mere resource— a subject for their experiments that was found to be useless. They had followed human satellites and space stations which led them to Earth. And they had determined that the planet would be stripped of resources and abandoned.

Those thoughts frightened Ali. If the aliens were left to thrive, there would be no hope left for humanity. All would perish. There would be no more humans. There would be no more animals or plant life. The aliens would take and slaughter all from the planet until nothing remained.

Ali shook his head. He refused to let that happen. If the burden he bore meant pushing himself to the limit to protect the entire world then he was prepared. He wished to solve the conflict with peace. But he knew if it came to it, fighting was going to be the only option.

The alien commander grumbled, "Wrong choice!"

While Ali contemplated how he was able to understand the alien's words, he felt a punch dig into his chest. His ribcage cracked and blood sprayed out of his mouth. The alien's punch hit harder than any bullet he had ever felt. His vision was faded from one direct hit alone.

Sore and weakened, Ali was unable to fight back as the alien grabbed him by his neck. His body flipped into the air as the commander swung him. Ali felt sick and dizzy, but he had no time to recover. The alien landed yet another punch and Ali struggled to remain breathing.

Blood dripped from his face. His wounds were deep. But he was healing. Ali was determined to outlast any blow— he had to. If he couldn't take on such a feat and challenge, he didn't know who else on Earth could. He would carry all of the Earth's pain himself. That was his burden.

The villainous fiend clutched Ali tightly and flew with him through the atmosphere. Dizzy, Ali struggled to comprehend what was happening before it was too late. He was being taken beyond Earth and into space. He gasped. Knowing that his powers were linked to the energy of the Earth, he knew it would mean his death.

Ali wondered if the alien knew of his weakness. He wondered if he had watched as Ali helplessly failed to reach the mothership as it orbited around the planet. Ali didn't know what to do. His strength had waned. He no longer had his powers while he was dragged through space. And he was struggling to breathe.

His vision was flickering like a flipbook. From his panic and the lack of oxygen, Ali feared he would suffocate and die. The alien, though, didn't seem patient enough to wait for that to occur. He winded up to land one final punch. And as Ali watched the beast's fist, he wondered if he truly was going to die.

But just before the alien could finish his attack, a green light surrounded Ali and created a shield. At last, he was able to breathe once more. But Ali had to wonder what had happened. He knew from the last time he tried to travel into space that his power had been drained. He wondered what was the source of this new green light.

The alien commander screamed as his fist smashed into the green shield. Ali remained unscathed, but as he checked the light around him, he noticed that it had dimmed after being struck. He feared that whatever this surge of energy was, it wouldn't last forever.

Punching the shield once more, the impact was enough to send Ali and the light floating across the moon's rocky surface. Without his powers to help him heal and withstand damage, Ali's bones were breaking. His flesh bled. And he felt himself getting weaker. He needed to fight back, but he didn't know how.

"Your power is connected to us," a voice said.

Ali darted his gaze but saw no one. As he focused, he recognized the voice to be the old woman, "This is as much as we can protect you. You will not be able to survive much longer."

Another blow sent him flying, but Ali wanted to continue listening, "I know that you do not wish to kill. So this is not an order."

It was as if Ali's mind was being taken over. He had flashbacks to his days in the army. The young Indian soldier's voice played in his mind— so frightened. The cries were unbearable for Ali. He wanted it to end. He held his hands over his ears and begged the voice to make it stop.

"Killing him wasn't to protect humanity. But if you fight this alien, you would be able to protect everyone you know and love."

Ali opened his eyes and saw a sword appear beside him. It was a manifestation of green transparent light. It glowed as bright as the crystal he recalled from the cave. If he took the sword, he knew he was meant to slay the alien. But the thought worried Ali. He still wanted there to be another way.

Saving humanity by causing more death was the last thing he wanted, but as he watched the alien commander, he saw that the fiend had summoned a long staff with a bright pink crystal. Whatever that weapon was, Ali didn't like the look of it. He couldn't stall any longer.

Pointing the staff at the green shield, it shot a ray of blinding light. Ali ducked as the shield shattered like glass. The green light had almost all but faded. And as parts of the beam penetrated his haven, Ali's skin was burned by the rays. He screamed as his flesh sizzled.

"When the cannons are ready, another one of your cities will be wiped off the face of the planet. And as you watch, you, too, will die a miserable death."

"No," Ali said, "I am the protector of Earth."

He could only assume the power of the green light allowed him to speak and understand the alien's language. That, or the alien had some way of speaking on his own. What was more important to him, however, were the images of his friends and loved ones. Back on Earth, there were people that were counting on him.

Every single human on Earth depended on him. Every soldier who fought the drones needed Ali to take down this fearsome foe. The UN members counted on him to buy them time. And he knew that back in Kashmir, his wife, children, and friends wanted him to return safely. *"That's right... I'm the protector of Earth."*

Ali reached for the sword. This was the final moment. He couldn't shy away from the burden any longer. As he touched the green light, the sword turned to metal. Power surged inside of Ali's body. He was ready. He made eye contact with the alien and he knew what he needed to do.

Leaping into the air, Ali was able to use the moon's limited gravity to soar above the alien's head. Focusing all of his weight downwards, Ali sliced the blade through the alien's head and down to his stomach. As blood gushed out of the foe, the alien was split in two.

Panting, Ali had used up much of his energy from the killing blow alone. Looking up at Earth, he didn't know how he would be able to reach it again. His body was burned and weakened. Even though the sword had filled him with power, he still couldn't fly all the way back to his home planet. But as he looked at the alien commander, he noticed the gold-plated suit that allowed him to fly.

SCENE XXIX

The city streets of Geneva were full of chaos. Not only did the drones threaten to melt and burn anything in their path, but small aliens from the mothership had landed to cause further destruction. Between the two forces, the soldiers were overwhelmed even with their numbers.

Troops from all around the world— from the Americas, Europe, Africa, Asia, and Oceania —were battling together to take out a common threat. Whatever weapons humanity had left was being used to fend off the attackers. But even united together, humanity was falling.

The drone missiles took out any soldier who tried to fire into the enemy hoards. Lasers melted flesh and bone. The thought creeping into everyone's mind was whether or not their efforts would be enough. They had yet to get any more readings from the mysterious man they saw and they wondered if he, too, had perished.

In the sky, the mothership had redirected and sat above Geneva. Watching the light above the cannons grow brighter, everyone knew that time was running down. What had happened in Shanghai would soon happen in their city as well. And this time, the worlds' armies would be completely wiped out.

Anna watched the satellite screen, "Where are you?"

A large blast alerted her. She switched the images on her screen and learned that one of their missile launchers had already been destroyed. Those were their last hope. Without those to shoot the mothership, they had no other weapons available to them left.

As she ran to the control room, she heard another blast. The second launcher had been destroyed. It was no use. The numbers of drones and aliens were too much for the armies to handle. They weren't able to hold them back and before long, the base would be in ruins.

"Protect the missile launchers!" A soldier screamed.

But just as he finished speaking, a third blast overtook him. The drones were relentless. They locked onto the launchers and destroyed them one by one until only a single launcher remained. Humanity was giving up hope. They needed a hero. And Ali was nowhere to be found.

Tears streamed down Anna's face as she cried, "We're doomed."

She watched in the monitor as a meteor barreled towards the city. She wailed. Geneva couldn't handle any more wreckage. This one last place would mean the end. As she closed her eyes, she expected the impact to be the very last thing she felt.

B-O-O-M.

Despite the shockwave, she was unscathed. Anna opened her eyes. On the monitor where the 'meteor' had crashed, she learned that it wasn't another alien attack at all— it was Ali.

His bones were broken and misaligned. Blood gushed from his lips. But as he felt the energy of the Earth around him, he began to heal. He crawled from the crater he created and attempted to reach the city above. Finally, he had made his way back to Geneva and he was determined to protect the world.

Soldiers watched in shock as Ali rose to his feet. All eyes were on him. Videos had spread of a man who flew and beat down drones like they were baseballs. Many believed it was all a hoax. They couldn't imagine that a real-life superhero was possible. But as Ali stood in front of them, they knew that he was real.

Ali closed his eyes and felt the wind around him. The army of whirling dancers— the green Darwaish — orbited around him. His power was returning. His wounds had all but healed. He could feel the pain and fears of everyone. He wanted to inspire them with hope. Ali opened his eyes. He knew it was time to fight and he believed he could do anything.

Back in the boardroom, another scientist put their hand on the woman's soldier, "We're not doomed yet."

With his sword in hand, Ali sped off with a sonic blast towards the drones. He sliced through them, sending shards of metal flying through the air. The Green Darwaish followed his movements. As he struck a single drone, a thousand members of his personal army were taking down more of the foes.

The aliens on the ground were in a panic. They shouted to each other and tried to regroup. For the first time, they were the ones frightened. And while they ran scared, the human armies were able to push back. Soldiers from all around the world worked together to take down a common threat.

On the mothership, the red light was growing bright. The cannons were almost ready. Watching from their screens, the aliens were ready to drop the final bomb that would reduce Geneva to ash. The only weapon standing against them was the four human missile launchers. And as they had learned, only one remained.

Workers flew down from the mothership, trying to take out the final launcher. As a fighter plane pilot watched, he tried to intercept them. But before he could fire their guns, the drones had locked on. Using their laser, the plane's wing melted and it plummeted to the ground.

Spinning out of control, the pilot shrieked in horror as he saw himself diving towards the final launcher. There was nothing he could do. The controls on the plane ceased to work. And the parachute wouldn't function. He closed their eyes just as the plane exploded, taking the missile along with it.

In the UN office, the team gasped. They had lost the last weapon they had that could take down the mothership. And they weren't the only ones left disappointed. The soldiers on the battlefield knew that the assault was over. With no other weapon that could put a dent in the ship, there was nothing more they could do.

And seeing the morale low, the aliens decided to take advantage of the situation. While the main cannons still charged, they sent small missiles to rain down on the city. It was their hope that they could take out the humans before they had a chance to regroup.

But humanity still had Ali. He and his green army rushed to the missiles. Using their long, flowing robes, the Darwaish caught the bombs and tanked the blast. Looking up at the sky, the human soldiers were finally able to see the army fighting alongside Ali. It was just as the legends from the sixties during the war between Pakistan and India— the green army was helping humanity.

The number of drones was finally dwindling. But the mothership was still the biggest threat. Ali knew if he didn't stop it soon, it would release a devastating blast that would destroy all life. He knew humanity had limited weapons left. But he had an idea.

Ali flew down to the road and found a tank. He knocked on the hatch and was greeted by a soldier. Shock overwhelmed the soldier. He squealed as he came face to face with Ali. Compared to himself, Ali was tall and muscular— ripped out of a page from a comic book. The young man was at a loss for words.

"You can fire this thing, right?" Ali asked.

As soon as the soldier nodded, Ali dropped to the base of the tank to lift it. But even with his overwhelming strength, he struggled. He needed more power. If he were to fly the tank into the air, he would need to gather more of the Earth's energy. So Ali closed his eyes.

"Are you sure?" the old woman asked.

It was as if she was appearing before his very eyes. The green light was swirling around him. She gazed at him. Her question held the weight of the world. She was offering Ali great power, but as he knew, the power came with a great burden.

No matter the cost, Ali knew he had to power through. Everyone and everything he knew and loved depended on his actions. Ali was prepared to do and give anything. Any pain was worth it to protect the world.

And Ali replied, "Yes. I am sure."

Power surged throughout his body. He felt his muscles bulge. He screamed aloud as he lifted the tank above his head. Bits of dirt and stone crashed to the ground. And only a cloud of dust was left in his wake as he blasted into the air towards the mothership.

It truly was the weight of the world that Ali held. As he soared into the air, it was as if his muscles were tearing apart. The pain radiated through his body, causing him to scream. But adrenaline kept him going. He knew he couldn't give up.

But Ali wasn't alone in his struggle. Alongside him, the Darwaish summoned tanks of their own. What began as just one tank multiplied to two. From two, it became four. And the multiplication continued until Ali's energy had summoned more than one hundred tanks.

The sky was filled with an entire fleet of flying tanks. He believed that if anything was going to take down the mothership, it was going to be this. And because time was limited, he knew his plan had to work.

With extra green energy flowing through his veins, Ali felt unstoppable. And what helped him was hearing the cheering voices of the soldiers below. Each of them watching believed in Ali and he refused to give up on them.

Ali knew that it wasn't just the soldiers that were watching him. With the satellites recording his every move, families around the world waited with bated breath. All of their survival depended on him.

Bursting forward, Ali lined himself up in front of the mothership. Rows of Green Darwaishs with their summoned tanks. If there was a greater force of power on Earth, he couldn't think of it. All of his fears subsided as he viewed the massive army on his side.

Inside the mothership, the aliens were in a panic. They knew what Ali meant to do and they had no means of retaliation. Their mouths went wide as Ali lined up the tanks around the ship so they were surrounded. From every angle, there was a tank ready to blast.

Looking down at the man in the tank, Ali knew that this moment was huge for him too. He wanted to give another human the honor of being a hero. This wasn't a moment just for Ali but for all of humanity, no matter who they were.

Ali smiled, "Fire!"

As the soldier launched a shell from the tank, tears of joy streamed down his cheeks. Thousands of tanks were firing at once. And the mothership's hard exterior cracked. As shards and fragments flew through the air, Ali knew humanity had won.

Like a sky of fireworks, metal bits burst into an array of vibrant hues. It was destruction and a celebration all in one. The windows of the ship cracked, sending aliens flying through the air. Sparks flew as the control systems short-circuited. And seeing every remaining bolt rain down to the Earth let Ali know that the ship was gone for good.

At last, humanity was saved. The threat against them was nullified. They no longer had to fear that the aliens would destroy them.

Landing back on the ground, Ali assisted the soldier out of the tank. He was in shock. And as his squad ran to him to cheer him on, he didn't have any words to say. The true hero was Ali. While no one truly knew who he was, they knew that without him, none of what happened would be possible.

The human armies were able to wipe out the remaining aliens that littered the streets of Geneva. After having their command station destroyed, the drones crashed to the ground. And with the city finally free of chaos, medical crews were able to sweep in to rescue any wounded soldiers.

Back in the boardroom, the scientists sent the footage of the mothership's destruction to every news and government agency in the world. Stations everywhere from Japan and Australia to South Africa and Brazil were celebrating the Earth's victory. The end of times had been averted.

Ali teleported into the UN office. The scientists stood in shock. He looked to the general who saluted and thanked him. Ali recalled that so many years ago he had been court-martialed. He was told that he was a disgrace. But on that day, he was respected by all of humanity.

Saluting back to the general, Ali glanced over at the screen. News and radio stations all over the world were reporting about him. They recognized that the world was saved by a man that the military in Pakistan called, 'Qalandar'. Ali smiled, and in a flash, he teleported away.

At last, he was back in Kashmir. He stood in front of his own home. His heart was pounding. After everything that had happened, he wanted to see his wife and children once more. He wanted to look them in the eyes, see their smiling faces, and tell them that they would always be safe.

In his garden, Ali spotted the rose bush. Though the snow still fell, a single red rose blossomed. It reminded him of Mehwish's rosy lips. He picked the flower and looked at the front door. She was in his heart the entire time he fought. He wanted to let her know how much she meant to him.

Scene XXX

> *"At the turn of every century, we tell ourselves that this time: there will finally be peace. But time and time again, war finds a war to tear us apart. So often, we seek out and find what makes us different instead of finding that which unites us."*

Ali's family sat huddled around the TV. When Saleem and Hassan had returned to tell them the news, they didn't truly believe that it was possible. But as they watched the videos on the news, they learned that Ali truly had gained power greater than any human had ever achieved.

> *"When all hope is gone, we often look for a hero to come. We wait for another to rescue us from despair. But rarely do we realize that each of us can*

> *be that hero. Each of us is capable of spreading love and life."*

The entire family felt hope and happiness pulsate through their hearts as they watched Ali lift the tank and fly into the air. He had truly become a superhero. It was as the army had stated. He was now 'Qalandar', the protector of Earth.

> *"No one wants to carry the burden that comes along with being a 'hero'. To truly fight for humanity is to sacrifice so much of one's self. We must be able to look at ourselves, accept our flaws, and strive to make the world a better place."*

Rabia pointed to the window, "Look, mama! It's raining flowers!"

Mehwish's soft green eyes widened. She stood and walked to the door. From the window, she could see the rose petals falling. And after all of the magic and mystery she had witnessed, she wondered if it could have been…

> *"When and if we can put our prejudices aside, we can finally hope to achieve peace. When we can look at every other human and give them the same love we wish to feel ourselves, peace is finally possible."*

Hiba and Fariha jumped up to follow her, but Hassan stopped them, "Let her go alone."

As Mehwish opened the door, she was mesmerised. Ruby red petals and snowflakes rained from the sky. She extended her hands to collect them. After all of the pain and destruction she had witnessed, there was finally beauty in the world again.

> *"God teaches us love. If we are to be thankful, we must be thankful to the world that God created. We must treat all that God has created with respect."*

Above her, Mehwish saw her husband flying down to her. He was hovering in the sky like a superhero. But she knew he was still Ali. He still had a warm and gentle heart. He protected all of humanity because he loved the world in which he lived. He cared about every human and animal. And most of all, he cared about his family.

> *"And if my acts today can teach humanity anything, it is my hope that we can all stay united. It is each of us coming together despite our differences that makes our world so beautiful."*

Ali brushed a rose petal from Mehwish's cheek. Tears welled up in her eyes. But they were tears of joy. Seeing his warm smile caused her heart to pound. She couldn't help but laugh. Looking up at him, she smiled with rosy lips that rivaled any rose petal that fell.

Epilogue

Most of the world was ready to focus on the future. With the threat of aliens freed from their lives, humanity was able to focus on everything they loved. Friends and family members celebrated that they could forever live peaceful lives.

Though, there was one person who still could not rest. Amma Ji sat in the cave twirling her staff. While everyone focused on the future, she could not help but consider the past. After all, she knew well that tragedy could strike at any time.

Wherever there was light, chaos was not far behind. Darkness always found its way to creep into anything. And that was exactly what the old woman feared. She worried that while the world rejoiced, a new threat would see it as an opportunity to strike.

Ali was everything bit of the superhero that the world called him, but his powers were still new to him. He knew what was needed of him when the time came. But Amma Ji still feared that his lack of experience would be his biggest detriment. Not only that, but with Ali's huge heart, he would have to handle the fact that even if he could save the world, he couldn't save every individual person in it.

Amma Ji thought back to a day long ago. There was an old, frail man with a white beard. He, too, wished for power like Ali. But both men were different. And while Ali wanted to give, the old man only wanted to take.

Greed was a dangerous thing. Amma Ji didn't know what the future held. Though, she knew it was far too soon to celebrate. At that moment, all she could do was pray and hope that the threat she feared would never return.